I0629051

DRAGONFOLD

And Other Adventures

By Tyrean Martinson

Copyright © 2013 Tyrean Martinson

Wings of Light Publishing

All rights reserved.

ISBN: 10:0988993317
ISBN-13: 978-0-9889933-1-0

DEDICATION

This collection of stories and poems is dedicated to every editor who said, "Yes!" and even to those editors who said, "No."

Plus, it's dedicated to all the my awesome blogging buddies who have inspired my writing with blog fests and encouraging words.

I give thanks and praise to God, my creator, for my imagination, and for all the undeserved blessings in my life.

CONTENTS

DRAGONFOLD

With her back against the sun-warmed stone wall of the garden, Azami fingered the fine paper in her fingers and slowly folded one edge and then another. Soothed by the smoothness of the paper, she could almost shut out the whine of her Aunt's voice in the dining room.

"No, no, no, we are seating twenty-four tomorrow night for dinner. Twenty guests and four family members, you fool, not just twenty," her Aunt screamed at the housemaid.

A hard slap echoed from the house, and Azami shivered. She sighed, as she saw the results of her reaction to her Aunt's temper: another damaged crane. It seemed she couldn't fold any of them right. Usually, she could fold anything she wanted, and the paper was a comfort to her hands. Today, it kept slipping and sliding away from her, getting crinkled on the edges, or not matching at the corners.

A long shadow fell over her legs, oddly lumpy in the middle. Late in the afternoon, even her pudgy Aunt could be tall with the sun at her back. "What have you done?! Can't you fold anything properly?! This is your wedding! You would think you could make a decent effort!"

"Yes, Aunt," Azami replied meekly. She knew it was no use to mention that the wedding wasn't her choice, and her cousin wouldn't notice if the cranes were folded properly or not. His greedy eyes would only be on the wedding feast.

"Hmmph! You'll have to go to the attic again, until your work is finished."

Azami swallowed nervously, "but Aunt, I will not have enough light to fold by —

"Nonsense! I've seen you fold better behind your back for the raggedy children in the village. Now get up!"

Azami quickly gathered her paper, keeping her eyes focused on her Aunt's lizard-hide shoes. "Yes, Aunt."

Her Aunt's long fingers with their spiked nails grasped Azami under the chin, pricking her skin. Azami was forced to look up slightly into her Aunt's fleshy face, and her hard cold eyes. "You will have those cranes finished by tomorrow morning, or I will teach my son how to whip you, before the wedding."

Azami felt her fear dissipate and her anger rise in her like a wave. "If he dares to whip me, I'll . . ." and the anger left her, as she belatedly realized that all her threats would be empty. After tomorrow her cousin would own her like a prize duck.

Her Aunt's grip on her chin tightened and her other hand raised and fell, striking Azami hard on the cheek. The blow was expected, but Azami could still not keep back the wash of tears that rose to her eyes.

"You will not threaten my son! You will obey him, and you will obey me! Now, to the attic with you!" Her Aunt's fat face had turned slightly purple with her rage, and she shoved Azami towards the house.

Walking quickly, Azami entered the overly warm house, and started up the staircase. The housemaid didn't look at her.

A door opened on the second landing, and her cousin's piggish face stared out at her. He leered, and she shuddered. He laughed, obviously enjoying her discomfort.

She scurried past him quickly, finally reaching the attic stairs. Holding the paper carefully she climbed up the narrow staircase, and entered the tiny attic door on her hands and knees.

She closed the attic door behind her and locked it. This place had been her prison and sanctuary for most of her life. Here, on a high ledge behind a loose brick in the chimney, she kept her private things. Here, she had learned of her gift; the reason that none of her folds could be perfect. If her Aunt discovered it, she would be locked in this attic day and night and forced to create things for her Aunt's pleasure and profit. It would be preferable to a forced marriage to her cousin, but she would not want to put anything under her Aunt's dominion.

And yet, here she was, trapped since all of her advocates were lost. Her mother had died of the fever when she was only seven, and then her grandmother had succumbed to old age just a year previously. The joint inheritance that she shared with her cousin would be lost when they wed; that was the real reason her Aunt had kept her under lock and key since Gramma's death. No other creature deserved such treatment, and so, her gift had to remain secret.

As if in response to her thoughts, she heard the purring of her kitten. He rubbed himself against her knee and placed a paw on her leg. She ran her hand over his head and back, and gazed into his beautiful green eyes. He was the first and only creature she had made on purpose. There had been others before, but they had been surprises to her, and thankfully had escaped before her Aunt had noticed them. The crane had flown away. The frog had hopped into the pond, and seemed content there.

Her kitten climbed into her lap and settled in, purring quietly against her stomach. Despite the hot humidity of the attic, she welcomed him. She leaned her head back, and let her kitten's contented rumblings soothe her. She let the paper fall from her hands, and daydreamed of being outside her Aunt's domain.

In the hazy mists of her dream, Azami looked on the gentle face of a man, glowing with white radiance. He held out his hands to her, and in them, he offered her the finest paper she had ever seen. She took it from him and he smiled broadly. She knew somehow, that he meant her to use her gift. He gestured with his hands, and she noticed the scars on them, as he seemed to indicate that she should fly away. In her dream, she almost understood, and she turned to float in blue skies.

With a start, she awoke to an angry pounding on the attic door. The kitten jumped from her lap, and she scrambled to her feet and made her way to the little door. "Yes, Aunt?"

She tried to open the door, but it was stuck, locked from the outside.

"You haven't finished those cranes, have you?"

"No, Aunt."

"Then I'll unlock the door tomorrow at dawn, and if they are finished, you'll have breakfast. If not, I'll have my son lay stripes on your back."

Azami shuddered. When she regained control of herself, she spoke again. "Yes, Aunt." Azami waited until she heard her Aunt's footsteps fade down the stairway outside. She gritted her teeth for a moment and then made a decision. She would not be whipped undeservedly. She would not subject herself to her Aunt's ways any longer. She would . . . what would she do? Feeling the soft paper in her hands, she suddenly knew. She would follow her dream. She would use her gift and fly away.

Walking softly and carefully, she crossed the attic and retrieved her precious possessions from their hiding place.

With sure fingers, she wrapped them into an old, frayed pillowcase that had served as some of her scant bedding when she had spent the night in the attic before. She also placed the paper inside it, keeping itself inside the pages of the scripture books that had been handed down to her by her mother. Not even the whole Bible, it still contained precious words of wisdom and comfort that had helped Azami keep her strength through the years. She remembered the night she had discovered her gift. Locked in the attic, dreaming a dream like the one she just had, she had woken to fold a scrap of paper she had been saving, and she had felt as if life itself had flowed through her fingers.

Calling her kitten with a soft clicking of her fingers on the floor, she picked him up and carried him and her pillowcase suitcase to the other end of the attic. There, a boarded up window had afforded her a view of the street. Tonight, she looked out, and made sure that there was no one on the street looking up at her Aunt's dilapidated roof. Putting her belongings down, she set herself to the task of loosening the boards on the window. It was a simple job, given that the roof was in need of repair. Her kitten jumped out of the window onto the porch roof, and started pushing at the boards to help her.

Finally, the window was open. Placing her bag of belongings carefully on the slanted roof, Azami squeezed herself through the opening. Taking a deep gulp of night air, she realized that she was afraid once again. She was crouched on the roof, and it felt precarious, as if any moment she might fall. She had never liked heights much. The kitten butted his head against her leg, and she took another gasp, afraid of losing her balance. Slowly and carefully she lowered herself to a sitting position on the roof.

Despite her fear of heights, her plan relied on her ability to handle them. That, and her gift. She didn't want to call it magic. It seemed like something else. She was creating something. She felt chilled at the thought of comparing herself in any way to the Creator of the Universe, but yet, she had always felt a call to create, even if it was usually only with paper. This was something more, as her warm and curious kitten proved to her one more time, as he poked his nose against her pillowcase.

She took out a single sheet of paper, and held it gently in her fingers. She bowed her head, and offered the paper upward. "Lord, please, accept this as an offering to you . . . this gift. It could only come from you, as all things created are from you, and blessed as good. Lord, please help me, and lend me your strength. Amen."

She lowered her hands, and closed her eyes, folding by feel and not by sight. She felt as if the Lord's power rested in her hands as she folded, filled with a love and a confidence that wasn't her own. Before the last fold, she hesitated. Silently she asked for confirmation that this was the right thing to do, that this work would be blessed. Then breathing deeply, and slowly, she carefully folded the soft paper one last time. She lifted the figure in her fingers, and blew her breath on it, and then reached her arm out to its full length and set the figure on the rooftop.

It quivered in the moonlight, and then the edges blurred and light surrounded it. Her kitten jumped into her lap, and she picked up her pillowcase. The light expanded a thousand fold, so that she had to look away. As the light receded she looked back, and there, with its claws gripping the roofing of her Aunt's house, stood her creation. The golden dragon inhaled heavily, and gazed at her, its eyes seeming to speak to her. She felt exhilaration course through her, and her fear vanished. The dragon bowed, and she bowed her head in return. Then the dragon turned slightly and knelt down.

With some hesitation, Azami put her hand out and touched the dragon. The dragon whuffed air into her hair, and she laughed. God had granted her this wonderful creation, why should she be afraid? She stepped gently onto the dragon's foreleg and climbed it carefully until she reached the dragon's shoulders. Once there, she seated herself with her legs rested on each side of the base of the dragon's neck. She tucked the pillowcase into her tunic, and the kitten made his way into her outer shirt and tucked himself against her stomach. She reached out and patted the dragon on its supple neck. The dragon turned its head and as Azami settled herself more firmly in place, gripping with her knees, she heard shrieks from below.

"What is that beast? What is it doing to my house?!" Her Aunt's nasally voice had reached a piercing tone. Her Aunt stood pointing upwards at them, accusingly.

"Dear, I think we don't want to anger it." Her Uncle, usually silent and unseen had stepped out onto the lawn, obviously restraining her Aunt from threatening the dragon.

The dragon huffed, obviously amused, and then stretching its wings, it began to beat the air, slowly at first, but then faster, and faster. Releasing its grip on the roof, it raised lurchingly into the air. After that Azami focused all her energy on hanging on with her legs and knees as the dragon worked its way upward with every wing stroke. They dipped, lurched, and then finally the dragon seemed to find a rhythm. Azami felt the dragon's muscles relax, and strain, relax and strain in a pattern that she could follow. Now she could look around her and down. Her Aunt cowered on the ground beneath her.

Azami noticed for the first time how tiny and pitiful her Aunt seemed, and her fear melted away completely. Never again would she have to suffer her Aunt's cruelty . . . or anyone else's for that matter. If she could fold a dragon, then who could hold her down? She was free. Free.

The dragon's flight swept them quickly away from her Aunt's house, but in the dark sky, Azami couldn't be sure where they were headed. Azami loved the feel of the wind against her skin, cold and refreshing. The dragon's warmth beneath her would keep her from getting too cold, and her kitten, with his claws clinging to her shirt, added more comfort. She realized slowly, with how bright the stars seemed and how small the lights below were, that she was much higher than she had ever been, and she wasn't afraid. It was a miracle. Freedom from fear, and freedom from her Aunt all in one day.

She closed her eyes, holding a strange sensation growing inside her. Strange and yet familiar, she slowly realized. She felt anticipation, the first she had felt in so long. It was strangely satisfying just to feel anticipation. If she could fold a dragon, and find freedom today, what would tomorrow bring?

She opened her eyes again. She had to hold this moment, capture it in her memory with reverence. The dragon's hide shimmered and even sparkled in the moonlight, and Azami looked up to the stars, noting their places. She couldn't remember most of the constellations, except the one she had learned from her mother . . . the cup. She searched the skies and finally she found it, and realized that they must be heading west.

Her mother had always told her that her past, and maybe even her future, lay in the west. The sea lay in that direction, and the mainland. According to her mother, she had been born on the mainland, in the Misty Mountains. It sounded like a fairy tale name, but she was sure that her mother had told her the truth. Maybe there she could find someone to explain what her gift meant, and how it worked so well. Maybe someone there would know her, or at least remember her mother.

For now, the dragon seemed to know where they were going, so Azami let herself revel in the flight. She was free, truly and wonderfully free. The stars in the sky stretched endlessly above her, and Azami felt as if her life looked as bright as the stars, for the first time in many years, she had hope.

THE IDENTITY CRISIS
OF CAPTAIN WRATH

Moonbeams shining eerily through clumps of clouds, a flock of water gulls skimming the rim of the Western Edge, sails taut against the wind and the Dauntless racing along the sea . . . it should have been exciting, but it wasn't. Not for Captain Wrath, aka Douglas Cranton, Jr., who had made this voyage every night for the last three lunar years.

He sighed to himself in his cabin, pouring over the passenger list. In the next few hours he had a burial at sea, a wedding, and a christening to perform. All of these duties, plus he needed to recite his stirring speech about the danger and excitement, the glory of life and death, and all that nonsense about living on the edge of the known world. It was all balderdash. Out of all the cruise ship captain jobs available to him after flunking out of the Royal Space Navy, he had landed this one. At the time, it seemed more exciting than the pleasure cruises to the "Forbidden" Isles.

Someone knocked on his door, and he welcomed the interruption. "Come in," he said in a low, booming voice that he adopted for his job.

"Sir, it's just me," said Telli, the cook, entering with a soft step and a discreet closing of the door behind her. Her face looked pinched with worry. "It seems we have a small problem with the wine we need for our three ceremonies and the finale speech."

Douglas groaned, and ran his right hand over his face with weariness and frustration. In his normal tone, he asked, "Would that small problem be Syparian Sea Slugs or Davies?" Davies, the first mate, had a penchant for alcoholic drink. In fact, he had been transferred from one of the Forbidden Isle cruises due to his inability to say no to wine or women.

"I think it's the slugs this time, sir," said Telli. "I put out the salt like you showed me and the beer traps . . . although I think Davies drank those." She looked uncertain for a moment, as if she shouldn't have said anything bad of Davies. Her background as a slave showed through sometimes.

"Telli," he said softly. "You are a better person than Davies ever will be. I trust your word over his any day."

"But if you should have to punish someone from the crew, to satisfy the role you play as Captain Wrath, I can take it."

"I'm still Douglas underneath all this," he growled, waving his hand over his ghastly makeup and heavy black beard.

"Sir!" she said sharply. "We need a Captain Wrath, and I think, if you don't mind my saying, that this ship runs better when you play your part."

He sighed, and stood, strapping on his double blaster belt, and his sword. Thankfully the blasted parrot had died last season and he didn't have anything on his shoulder squawking in his ear.

Outside his cabin, Doug took on the role of Captain Wrath for the sake of the paying passengers. He stomped in his heavy black boots, swore at the crew but not Telli, and threw open the door to the ship's mess with a thunderous bang. Once there, he slammed the door shut behind him, and then walked quietly to the wine cellar. The salt circles around the bottles were still intact. There were no slime trails, but there were little foot prints, and he thought he saw movement out of the corner of his eye. He turned quickly, and overturned a few of the rum jugs in his haste, grabbing at a pair of legs.

The little being struggled in his grasp for a moment, and then became quiet with affronted dignity. It appeared to be a very small man dressed in green. "Unhand me at once, you oaf," he shouted squeakily.

"What the devil!" shouted Doug, not even having to try for his Captain Wrath impersonation this time. He glared at the little man, and gave him a small squeeze. "I don't recall any Leprachanarian on my passenger list!"

Doug felt little pinpricks of pain on his ankle and looked down to see a horde of the tiny little people stabbing him with their tiny knives.

"Stop, or I will stomp on you," he shouted. "You're all charged with trespassing, assault, and damages to Universal Cruise Lines." Then with the hook on his left hand he fumbled with his com button. "Cookie, get in here. We have stowaways aboard," he snarled. "Bring a sack."

"A sack, sir?"

"We have an infestation of Leprachanarian trespassers," he growled.

"We'll give you our gold," said the little man in his hand.

"I'm not falling for that one," said Doug. "Your people are the reason I was thrown out of the Royal Space Navy."

"You're Doug Cranton?" the little man peered at him, with a smile at the corner of his mouth. "That Doug Cranton?" He started to giggle.

"I'm Captain Wrath aboard this ship," snarled Doug. "Don't you forget it."

"That's right," said Telli, from behind him. She smiled at him, and then using a broom and a catchall bag, she swept up the other Leprachanarians in one swooping blow.

"Nice work, Cookie," Doug said. "Now, throw them in the bilge with the rats, and find us some drink in the cargo hold. We have paying passengers to attend to before the moon sets."

"Yes, sir," she said, seriously, and then she winked. "Nice to have Captain Wrath aboard tonight."

FIERCE LOVE

Wings of an eagle
with a lion's claws
Ultimately regal
with soft paws

He sees his prey
under the house eaves
and he waits for the end of day
nested in a bed of leaves.

She stands by her window
glaring out at the night,
grieving with inner cold,
failing to see the light.

With a sweep of air
He sends leaves fluttering,
her eyes grow wide with fear

and a spell of anger, she is muttering.

But he stops the spell,
with the warmth of his breath
flowing through every cell
he frees her from certain death.

Newborn with wonder
free to see the bright heaven
she knows the love of a savior
and shines like a beacon.

NEW GROWTH

The trees reached downward bending away from the wind. They overlapped just enough to protect Sage from the elements without, and she wished they could protect her from the elements within. Sorrow and anger washed over her, and she dug her hands into the rich soil and pine needles matted underneath her.

The soil, full of small living creatures, thrummed a steady comforting hum of life. Dying leaves and needles nourished the new seeds germinating under the soil. So much hope and renewal just under her fingertips, and Sage drew from it, slowly at first, easing her headache. As that hope flowed freely into her, she channeled it to heal the tension in her body, and almost healing the anger and pain in her heart.

Suddenly, a loud screech interrupted her, and several points of pain erupted in her shoulders as something heavy and taloned landed on her back. She struggled to pull herself away from the animal. As she turned, an enormous owl flew away from her and landed on nearby stump, eyeing her angrily.

"What?"

"The same question I might ask you," intoned a deep voice above her head. "What do you think you were doing taking the forest's life to ease your own heartache?"

Sage searched the overhead tree limbs, but couldn't spot the owner of the voice. "Who are you?"

A slight movement in the high branches of a nearby fir tree caught her attention. She could almost make out the figure of a man, next to the trunk.

"Answer my question and I may answer yours."

"I hurt, and the land has healing powers. All know this." Sage directed her words at the place where she thought the man stood, up in the fir tree.

"And can all take the life of innocent creatures to ease their own small pains?" With a gentle leap and a soft thump, the man landed next to her, piercing her with his sharp gaze.

"I didn't . . .I wasn't," Sage started to defend herself, but then she placed her palm to the ground and realized that she where she lay, the forest plants were dying. The tiny green shoots were wilted. She hung her head in shame. "I didn't think my need would dent the strength of the forest." It seemed she was doomed to make mistakes she couldn't mend.

The man, dressed all in browns and mottled greens, put down his staff, and reached his hand down to the earth.

Sage felt the small seedlings heal, and felt their life. "How did you do that?"

"I gave of myself, and of the energy of the elder trees." He gestured towards the tree he had been in earlier. He shrugged. "I actually could have done that all from my perch, but I wanted you to feel it, and know, really know, that you can affect the life around you."

Sage felt a small stirring of hope inside herself. "Could you show me how to do that? How to fix things?"

"Yes."

"Will you show me now?" Sage knelt in front of him, pleading. "I made a mess of things earlier today, and I really need to fix something." Sage felt her face get warm with embarrassment and shame.

The man knelt beside her. "Tell me."

Sage wished she could hide from his piercing gaze, but she couldn't. He could help her set things right. "I accidentally set some ivy on a girl in my village, and . . . it wouldn't stop growing."

He gave her a very stern look. "I will help her, and then I will speak to your parents."

"They disowned me. The village threw me out. They might take me back if you help though. They thought I was a . . . witch."

"Let's go then." He stood and started walking in the direction of the village.

"How do you know the way?" she asked him, running to catch up.

"I'm a forester, and I sensed something wrong in the forest in that direction."

Within a short time they passed the outer fields, and then entered the empty village square. He led them back along the steps she had taken to the forest, and right into lover's lane – a lane with flowering branches intertwined overhead that led to a small pool fed by a rushing waterfall. On the left of the pool a crowd of sobbing women and men armed with pruning shears surrounded Calliope and Kyle, who were both encircled by ivy up to their waists, with its growth only stemmed by the busy shears.

The forester didn't bother speaking to any of the villagers, but simply brushed past them to lay his hands on the lowest growth of the plant.

Calliope's father gestured at him with the shears, but stopped when he saw the vines wilting away from his daughter and Kyle. Calliope stepped free of the vines and into her mother's embrace, tears tracking down her face. Kyle and Calliope's father turned to the stranger, who stood, holding a small ivy rootlet in his hands.

Calliope's father recovered from his shock faster than anyone else around him. "Thank you, stranger. My daughter . . . well, my daughter owes you her life. You are welcome to stay at our house this evening if you wish, and I will find some way to repay this debt."

"No need," the stranger replied. "I am a forester. It is my duty to care for the green, living things, and all that rely on them. I require only the life of this plant, and the bond of this girl, as my thanks." He gestured to Sage as he said this.

The others seemed to notice her for the first time, and their faces furrowed, and darkened with anger.

"Please, I'm so sorry. Please. . . I didn't mean for anyone to be hurt." Sage pleaded with them, looking at Calliope and Kyle, and then her parents. Kyle wouldn't look at her, and her parents turned their backs on her. She felt as if her heart would break.

Only one person seemed to notice her, and she was the last one that Sage wanted to speak with. Calliope's white face burned red. "You! You . . .," her voice trailed away as if in fear.

The forester stepped closer to Sage's parents. "Your daughter's bond?"

"We have no daughter," her father stated.

Calliope's father stepped forward, "now, Olsen, I have the right to be angry, but I know she is just a youngling, and younglings do make mistakes."

Her father glared at Calliope's father, and then turned to face the forester, still not looking at Sage. "You may have her bond. I will sign it."

"Thank you," the forester replied. "I must ask for just one more thing however. If she may retrieve her personal effects and a change of clothing suitable for traveling in all weathers, I would appreciate it."

Sage's father nodded curtly. "My wife will prepare her things. We will meet you in the village square."

"If it must be so, then it shall be," the forester said sadly.

"What will you do with the ivy?" Calliope demanded.

"I will plant it far from here, where it can grow without fear or menace," the stranger gently replied.

"Thank you," Calliope said. She turned to look at Sage, and her face paled and then became stern. She crossed the small space between them and held out her hand. "I accept your apology Sage."

"You do?" Sage couldn't believe Calliope would forgive her so easily, when her parents wouldn't.

"You apologized, and it is my duty to forgive."

"Oh," Sage felt disappointed somehow and yet relieved that her enemy was only being dutiful.

Then Calliope leaned a little closer to her, and gave her a knowing look. "Besides, I can afford to be forgiving when I have won Kyle, and you are going to suffer the consequences for your actions."

Sage felt anger well up in her, but before she could even think of doing anything, the stranger was at her side, with a hand on her shoulder.

"Think before you act. This is your first lesson." His blue eyes pierced her.

Sage felt ashamed of her impulsive anger. "Yes, sir." She dropped her gaze, not wanting to look at him.

He removed his hand from her shoulder, and took one of her hands in his own, turning it so that her palm faced upward. Then he placed the small ivy plant in her palm. "This shall be your reminder until we leave."

Sage felt her cheeks redden, and her throat felt constricted with tears. She stood staring down at the plant, while the others talked and walked away. Finally, she thought she was alone, and she looked up.

Kyle stood there, his red-brown hair glinting in the sunlight. "Sage, I never meant to hurt you. I don't understand what you did, and I think it was wrong, but I know you didn't mean to hurt Calliope or me." He stated this with complete assurance.

Sage looked away, unsure if she agreed with him. There had been a moment, when she had caught them kissing by the pool, when she had wanted Calliope to hurt as badly as she felt hurt.

"I think you will do well with this forester. He can teach you . . . the things you need to know about . . . well, about what you do. You know, I've known about it for a long time. I saw you growing Widow Junson's roses. That was very kind of you."

"Kind, but too strange, right?"

Kyle shifted uncomfortably. "That's not why . . . well, why I care for Calliope. You need to be out in this world, and this is my place, this village and the fields around it. I fit here, and Calliope fits with me."

Sage looked up at him. He was trying so earnestly to be kind to her. It was one of the things she had always loved about him. "I understand, Kyle. I hope . . . I hope you have a good life with . . . with Calliope."

"Thanks." Kyle placed his sun-browned hand on her shoulder for a moment and gave her a gentle squeeze. He smiled at her, and then turned to walk after the others.

Sage watched him go, and felt struck again with heartache as she saw him place his arm around Calliope's shoulders. Calliope leaned into him, and Sage sucked in her breath and stared down at the ivy rootlet in her palm. It was so fragile, just like her place in her own village had turned out to be.

As she waited in the village square for the forester and her parents to come, her sense of isolation deepened. No one seemed to want to even look at her, much less speak to her. Sage leaned against the well for support, and stared down at the rootlet, as if it might solve the pain in her heart. She heard quick, small footsteps, but she didn't look up until a warm bundle of legs and arms had collided into her.

Her sister, Faith, wrapped her legs and arms around Sage's waist, and looked up at her with sad, puppy-like eyes. "Don't go away, Sage, please don't."

A yawning chasm of grief opened in her stomach, and Sage grappled with her own need to sorrow and her sister's need for comfort. "I'm so sorry, Faith, but it's not my choice. I have to go."

Faith buried her face against Sage's stomach, and mumbled something.

Sage knelt down, and gently put her arms around her sister, holding her against her shoulder, and smelling the sweet flowery scent of Faith's hair. "Oh, little sister. I am going to miss you the most."

"And I'm going to miss you Sage. Why did you have to go and do something bad to Calliope?"

"I lost my temper, and I didn't know it would be that bad." Sage sighed. "I hope you'll forgive me, Faith."

"I forgive you. But I wish you didn't have to go away. You are coming back, aren't you?"

"Yes. I promise that I will do everything in my power to come back. You are my lovey little sis, and I'm not going to live my whole life without you."

"Your whole life?"

"I'll have to be gone for a while before Mum and Dad forgive me."

"Not longer than a month, right?"

"Probably longer than that."

Faith clung to Sage, and started to sob. Sage started to cry as well. Belatedly, she realized, her ten-year old sister meant more to her than anyone else in the world did. She had cared for Faith as a baby, as a toddler and had played with her as she became a youngling. Her act of anger and selfishness had wrenched them apart.

She heard a loud grunt above them, and she looked up to see her father standing above them. His expression looked pained. "I have your things."

"Thank you, Da." She felt tears continuing to track down her cheeks.

His face tightened, and he cleared his throat loudly. "This is the best thing, Sage. You have to go away from here. You could become a criminal without the right training, and I think this forester's got the right ideas. I don't like . . . well, I don't like your 'gift' as he called it, but it's not unexpected." His voice quieted to a whisper. "My Grandmother and her people had a strangeness about them. The village here, and Mum, well, they won't be comfortable around you anymore."

"But disowning me, Da?"

"I'm talking to you aren't I? Just keep your visits quiet, and you can see Faith once or twice a year. Send a message ahead to give us warning."

Faith stood up and glared at Da. "Only once or twice a year? How could you Da?"

"It is what is best, and I don't want to hear any more about it, or any talk about my Grandmother's family either."

Faith looked rebellious, and then glared up at him again. "What if I get strange too, Da, are you going to send me away?"

"Heaven forbid." Da's face took on a new look of forbidding concern.

A shadow fell over Faith and Sage looked up to see the forester.

He cleared his throat and quietly stated. "She will be gifted, sir. I see it in her."

"Isn't there a way to stop it?"

"No, and trying to just might make it worse when it comes. I think that is partly the case for Sage. She has been repressing her gift for a long time."

"Then if I have to go away, I want to go now, with Sage." Faith looked stubborn.

The woodsman almost smiled. "You are a very brave girl, and in some places that would be acceptable. But here and now, it is not a good idea. Your father needs you, and your mother too. You still have plenty of learning to do in the school here in your village. We all have gifts, but some are more noticeable than others. We will return for visits, and to check on your gift's progress. When it is time, you will either join your sister and I, or we will find you a teacher."

"Thank you." Faith reached out and shook the forester's hand. "Faith Olsen."

The forester smiled broadly. "Pleased to make your acquaintance, Mistress Faith. I am Laurent Hawkins, your sister's new Master Teacher."

"Do you mean that I'm apprenticed, or bonded?" Sage asked. Apprentices had training, while bond slaves had only labor. She didn't want to be a bond slave, but knew that she deserved that kind of punishment.

"Both." Laurent stated. "You will have time to read the contract at our first campsite." He looked at Faith's father and nodded. "It is a fair agreement, and your parents did well by you, even if your actions warranted something harsher."

Sage didn't say anything, not sure what could be harsher than being disowned by your own family.

"For now, you must say your goodbyes, for we have several miles to travel today before we camp. I am on an errand."

"Yes, master Laurent." Sage stated dutifully.

Her Dad handed her a satchel that fit on her back, and handed her a pair of leather boots. "You'll need these for the journey."

Sage took them with surprise, for although they were working boots, they were obviously crafted in her size. The shoemaker must have made them in the last few weeks. "Thank you, Da."

Her Dad shrugged. "You're welcome. Now, no sooner than a fortnight. Come along Faith."

Sage ached to hug her father, but she knew he would not allow it, not after publicly banishing her. Faith turned and gave Sage a big kiss on the cheek and a hug.

"I love you."

"and I love you. God Bless your days Faith."

"And yours."

And then they were walking away, Dad's hand on Faith's drooping shoulder.

Master Laurent touched her arm for a moment. "Time to go."

"What about my shoes?" Sage indicated her sandals and the boots in her hands.

"You may change them at our first rest. It's time for you to leave this place now." He gestured around them. "One last look, and then take a breath and let it all go."

It hurt too much to see the villager's anger, so she simply breathed in and out and then followed him, a half step behind, like any apprentice or bonded slave would do, out of the village, at a fast walk. She wondered if Master Laurent ever went anywhere slowly.

To her surprise, the first place they stopped was the small clearing where they had met.

Laurent drew a small circle in the dirt with his foot, and then waved his hand towards it. "Here is where you shall put your rootlet, and we shall return here to see how it grows."

Sage felt another wave of despair wash over her. "Master Laurent, must we return here?"

"It shames you?"

"Yes."

"Good. I do not want you to wallow in your despair, but you must learn, and this lesson is an important one. You have to repent, accept forgiveness, forgive yourself, and grow. We all have a starting place, a seed that starts us on our journey. This one represents yours. Plant it, and eventually it will be a source of strength and not of shame."

Sage knelt on the ground and scooped up dirt with her hands. When the hole was large enough, she placed the ivy rootlet tenderly in it, and covered it gently with earth. Somehow, sitting there in the dirt, it looked as forlorn and out of place as she felt. She raised a hand over it, and then paused to look up at her Master Teacher. "May I?"

"Just a touch, to help it start."

She concentrated, and instead of pulling energy out of the earth, she pulled some of the life inside herself and gave it to the tiny plant, making sure it took root in the soil, and had enough nourishment for a day or two. When she opened her eyes, it hadn't grown much, but she could see it was standing straight.

"An excellent start." Her teacher stated warmly.

BATTLE CALL

Weariness clashes
With vigorous sword strokes that
Beat down enemies

Opponents silenced
The warriors pause, swords dropped
Waiting for the horn

Robust but hollow
The bellow releases them
Until the next call

ENOUGH TO DO

Joanna woke, and found her gaze resting on the open door across from her. Filled with the green of spring, highlighted by flowering vines and blue sky, the doorway invited her forward.

She closed her eyes, and turned her back on it, letting a sob rise up in her throat before pushing it down again.

A shuffling of footsteps warned her of a visitor, and she forced herself to relax.

A soft hand touched her shoulder, followed by Nana Clerina's rasping old voice, "You have to get up someday, Joanna, and today is as good a day as any."

Joanna stiffened, feeling the coldness in her heart seep into the outermost layers of her skin, betraying her wakefulness. "No," she said, keeping her eyes shut.

"The pain is only going to lessen with time, and with life. If you lay here like one of the dead, it will only consume you, child," Nana stated firmly.

Joanna ground her teeth together, and pulled her shoulder away from Nana's touch. "I should have died," she said.

Nana sighed long and deep, and then was silent. Her shuffling footsteps carried her away, towards that doorway of green and light. Her footsteps paused for a moment, and she said, "there is a purpose for every life, child, even one as old as my own, or as heartbroken as yours."

Joanna waited until the footsteps died away, and then she opened her eyes to stare at the blank wall of her cell. It had been her room once, filled with art, music, and the laughter of friends. She had ripped the artwork from the walls, destroyed her flute, and thrown the bedding outside the first day she had returned home. Now she lay on a hard bed frame, with only her cloak wrapped around her. Suddenly, she realized she was missing something. What could it be?

She sat up, and looked around her, quickly alert, reaching for . . . nothing. She slumped in her seat, bowing her head over her knees. Her sword had been broken. Her right arm ended in a stump, healed at Nana's expert touch but not whole. Never whole again. The enemy had left her for dead, and she might as well be with no hand, and no sword. Her country had been defeated by a bunch of bandits, her friends had been killed or taken away. She shuddered to think of how those bandits might have used them.

Waking on the battlefield, with a crow pecking at her stump, and the bodies of her comrades strewn around her, she had only one thought . . . to escape the horror that surrounded her. So she had run home, taking the back trails to avoid people, and now the horror still lived with her in her head. She couldn't stop seeing the images of that gore-covered battlefield. She knew their country stood on the edge of destruction by the bandit hordes, and yet she hoped that somehow their small village would be overlooked.

A feeble scream interrupted her thoughts. The sounds of a struggle were unmistakable, and Joanna leaped to her feet, and grabbed the water jug that Nana had left for her. Stepping close to the wall, she peered out the doorway to see Nana on her knees, grappling with a bandit who had a hold of her long white hair. Another bandit stood laughing, while he watered their horses in the courtyard fountain. Their high, clicking speech made no sense to Joanna, but she could tell that they were being crude just by the expressions on their faces.

What could she do? There were just two of them, it seemed, probably stealing necessities for their forces. She glanced about her room. She really had thrown out everything. The water jug was her only weapon. However, just outside the door, Nana's garden hoe lay in the dirt. Quietly, she put down the jug, and softly stepped into the courtyard. Focused on their sport, the bandits didn't seem to notice her. She knelt and picked up the hoe, and then sprinted across the courtyard, screaming at the top of her lungs, startling both men and their horses.

Instead of attacking the bandit by the fountain, she brought the hoe down on the reins that he held, then smacked the horses with it as well. The horses panicked, and ran. The bandit stumbled, and she launched herself at him, knocking him into the fountain with the momentum of her body. He floundered, thrashing around, and she held onto him, pushing him under.

Behind her, Nana screamed again, and Joanna turned just in time, and moved to the side as the other bandit brought down his sword, narrowly missing her but mortally stabbing his friend.

Joanna backed up, looking around her for an idea, or a weapon. As she looked, Nana ran to the kitchen alcove, and the bandit yanked his sword out of his friend's body. He looked stricken, and enraged. Bellowing he threw himself towards her, with his sword high.

Joanna couldn't believe he was that stupid. It was if time slowed, as she stepped to the side of one of Nana's planters, and as he rushed her in the narrow space, she ducked, slid and tripped him, letting his rushing weight carry him into the side of the toolshed. Then Nana was at her side, offering her a kitchen knife. Joanna took it, weighed it in her left hand and threw it, striking the bandit in the chest as he rose to attack again.

He fell backwards, tripping over a shovel, his sword dropping from his fingers.

Joanna stepped forward, took the sword in her left hand, and with a swiping side cut across his throat, she killed him.

Standing there, over the still body, she knew her purpose. Nana healed. She fought and killed, in defense of her people. She didn't like the blood. She didn't like death. But when she fought, everything came into place.

"There may be others," Nana said quietly.

"They only send out small groups to attack homesteads and villages. There will be more in town," Joanna said. She looked at Nana, measuring the toughness of her grandmother for the first time. Despite the attack, Nana looked strong. "You can bring your herbs, and I will bring this," she said, holding the sword up, "and we can help. The bandit leader, Van Dalsing, will have only sent a dozen to our village, because he will think it of no consequence. We will teach him otherwise."

"And then?"

Joanna took a deep breath. "Then, we will have to plan for tomorrow. But today, we have enough to do."

AT THE EDGE

Shari wasn't the chosen one. She didn't have to be at the cliffs at dawn. Not like her best friend Kyrie did. But she couldn't let Kyrie die. Kyrie had a family, and a boyfriend. Vibrant, and full of hope, Kyrie had held up their village during the Longest Night when the Night Storms had taken half of their cattle and some of their strongest warriors.

Shari didn't have anything to lose, and she wouldn't be missed by anyone, other than Kyrie. That's why she had to break the law, and sacrifice herself before Kyrie could reach the cliffs.

She had snuck out of the orphan house in the middle of the night, dressed warmly against the freeze, and crept her way through the silent village streets. Skirting around the Protectors had been easier than she expected, but she supposed that they were meant to keep the Night Storms out, not keep people in.

At the cliffs she waited until the earliest streaks of light stretched across the sky. She could hear the official procession coming through the village, and she knew she had to time this just right. They had to see her jump, so they would know that the sacrifice had been made. Kyrie would be safe then.

When the procession drew nearer, Shari could just make out the faces of those in the front line. The village headman, chief of the Edge Clan, Ghanto Trevayn, had a wrinkled brow, and a sour tilt to his mouth. Leaning heavily on his staff, he kept glancing at Kyrie and the Protectors that walked with them. He didn't look too happy about the choice of sacrifice either. No one could be, except perhaps, the Protectors. The Protector's faces were almost identical and without expression. They were taller than the Edge clan by at least an arm length in height, and their black armor melded into the darkness so that their faces appeared to float in the dimness.

Kyrie had the red hood of the Sacrifice robe over her head, but Shari could just see the firm set of her lips, and the tightness in her cheeks.

They had come close enough, Shari realized. She stepped out of her hiding place by the jumble of rocks by the Sacrifice platform. Her heart pounded wildly in her chest, and her mouth was dry. Somehow, she managed to croak out her final words.

"This Sacrifice is not needed. I volunteer as Sacrifice in her place."

They didn't appear to hear her.

So, she sucked in air, and shouted out, "This Sacrifice is not needed. I volunteer as Sacrifice in her place."

The procession stopped.

Kyrie whipped off her hood, and cried, "No."

The Protectors stepped forward, pulling their bows off their shoulders.

She didn't have time to say goodbye.

Shari turned on her heel, and leapt out into the rays of dawn that lit up the canyon below her.

She screamed, and flailed in the emptiness, feeling the wind pressing up all around her.

Suddenly, a dark shape flew beneath her, and she landed in a heap on the back of Night Storm.

She wanted to push it away, and push herself off into the abyss, but she found herself clutching at its feathers.

"Stay still, girl, your sacrifice has just begun," whistled its voice.

As the giant owl-woman flew over the canyon, Shari shivered and pressed herself closer to the creature's back. Surprisingly, the Night Storm didn't smell like rotting carrion as the lessons had said they would. It actually smelled of fresh air. Of course, that could be because they were flying.

They were flying. Shari repeated this thought to herself, and decided that no matter the outcome of the flight, whether the Night Storm decided to sacrifice her in some bizarre ritual or just eat her alive as the legends suggested, she would enjoy this moment of flight. It wasn't something that people got to experience otherwise.

She raised her head just a little at first, and opened her eyes slowly. She had to keep them slitted because of the pressure of the wind in her face.

The Night Storm flew swiftly over the canyon with rhythmic beats of its wings, and the canyon walls were beautiful in the morning light. The reddish soil that made the rocky cliffs also had orange, brown, and even black streaks throughout them.

Shari had never been in the canyon before, so the scenery was fascinating. She hadn't known that trees and bushes could cling to the sides of rock, or that there was a river far below them. She forced herself to look down until she started to feel dizzy, and then she quickly turned her gaze forward.

The Night Storm seemed to be flying toward a particular outcropping of rock that stood high above all the other outcroppings, centered in the widest part of the canyon.

If that was their destination, then her end might be near. She had to make the most of this moment. Slowly, Shari sat up on her knees, balancing easily on the Night Storm's back.

"What are you doing, sacrifice?" the owl's head of the creature swiveled to eye her warily.

"I want to . . .to feel the wind, once more at least," she said.

The owl's eyes contracted slightly narrowing the pupil, and the bird made a thrumming sound in its chest. Then it shook its head slightly and simply said, "Just don't even think about jumping off."

"Never," Shari said. She put her arms out one at a time, and let the wind run over her hands and arms. It felt delicious and wonderful. After this, she figured, she wouldn't mind dying so much.

After several minutes, the Night Storm looked back at her again and said, "time to tuck in now, before I land. I don't want to lose you."

"All right," Shari said, and she obliged, nestling down against the Night Storm's back. She wondered that a creature that she had been raised to fear could be so . . . unlike anything she had expected.

PTW FRED

Once upon a time, a Prince of Technical Wonders of the 3rd kind, otherwise known as a "self-made" man with all skills mechanical, and electrical, wandered into a village inn and heard an unlikely tale of a Princess captured by an evil wizard and held captive behind The Hole-in-the-Wall.

Now, as our Prince of Technical Wonders, hereafter referred to as PTW Fred, was chilled from a motorcycle ride through a rain forest, he was ready for some hot java, and thought he might as well listen to this outlandish tale.

The teller of said tale was a young man dressed in a torn rayon shirt, with ragged designer jeans flapping around his ankles. He looked wind-beaten and sunburned and held a mug of espresso clenched between cold-reddened hands.

"I'm telling you, I was attacked by the evil wizard's minions, so many that I could not count them. Some had multiple arms, and tentacles, and some had razor sharp weapons, you see what they did to me?" the tale-teller whined. He held up one of his sandaled feet, which was scraped and bleeding.

The barista made some appropriate noises of shock.. "I'll get you a warm wash cloth for your wounds, sweet Prince." She smiled her dimples at the young man.

"Prince?" PTW Fred asked, feeling that if he didn't assert himself soon, he would never get a cup of coffee.

"Don't you know who he is?" the barista asked, and then answered her own question, "He's Prince Cale, the Prince of the Southern Beachlands."

Prince Cale stood, with obvious pain from the scrapes on his feet, and held out his hand to PTW Fred. "And you are?"

"I'm Fred, Prince of Technical Wonders of the 3rd kind." When this brought only puzzlement to their faces, he added, "I work with electronics mainly, and once did a stint with a power company, in the transmission and distribution department."

"Oh," Prince Cale's brow furrowed in thought. "Doesn't that actually make you a wizard?"

"Well, my father was a King, and Prince Wizard Fred, or Wizard Prince Fred doesn't work well as a title."

"Oh, maybe you could save the Princess!" the Barista

looked thrilled by this news, and leaned forward eagerly, "what would you like to drink?"

"I'll have a Latte, please."

As the barista left, Prince Cale leaned forward conspiratorially; looking to make sure none of the other baristas heard him. "You know, you might want to make your future drink orders more complicated. They expect that from a prince, and," he winked, "it keeps them wondering what you'll order next."

PTW Fred simply let the advice sink in, and then he let it go, with a short nod. He settled himself down onto a nearby stool, not wanting to get the cushier armchairs wet with his soggy clothing. He shivered momentarily, and noticed Prince Cale eyeing him.

"So, what's your tale, Prince Fred?"

"Nothing very exciting. Just a wet ride on a motorbike through the rainforest."

"Ooh, you have a motorcycle?!" a different barista, this one with long dark ringlets hanging over her shoulders, cooed at him. "I love men who ride motorcycles." She put her hand on his arm. "Tell me about your ride . . . was it exciting?"

"Umm," Fred was taken aback by her response. "I think Prince Cale's story sounded more intriguing than my own, if you don't mind. I would like to hear more."

"It would be my pleasure," Prince Cale stated in a satisfied voice, as the baristas leaned toward him. "Although it is a tale of pain and suffering, I am glad to tell it, as a warning to those who might cross the evil wizard from the Hole in the Wall." He fussed with his bedraggled golden curls for a moment, and then began his tale, with his hands around his mug.

"As I said earlier, once upon a bright morning on this beautiful northern beach, I thought I heard a maiden singing. Her voice compelled me with its beauty, and I thought . . ." he sighed dramatically, "I thought I was soon to meet my match, my princess. But I was wrong." He took a sip of his java, and then gave Fred a compelling look. "One must be careful of the type of maiden one acquires as a bride, these days. You never know what her family background might be like."

The baristas around Prince Cale stiffened, and stepped back, as if dealt a blow.

"I think I see one of our regulars coming up the walk,

Sally," the ringlet haired girl stated.

"Yes, and I have something that needs tending to in the back," Sally stated.

Prince Cale looked surprised. "Ladies, don't you want to hear the rest of my tale?"

"We have a business to tend to, sir." The brunette stated firmly.

Fred held back a laugh, as he watched Prince Cale's face become dismayed.

"But who's going to get me a warm-up?" he held up his cup plaintively.

"I think Cassie will be back in just a moment from her break. I'm sure she can tend to you." Sally stated over her shoulder as she made her way back to the espresso bar, and busied herself behind the machine.

Prince Cale watched them for a moment, and then turned to Fred. He shrugged, obviously bemused. "Women, you just never know what they're thinking."

"Obviously not," Fred couldn't help stating, with a smirk on his face. He wondered how many women Prince Cale had frightened off with his arrogance. "However, I would still like to hear of this Hole in the Wall adventure and the evil wizard. I might be able to do something . . . or at least call someone who could." He pulled out his spell-phone and held it up for a moment.

Prince Cale pulled out his own spell-phone, a brilliant bright blue one with purple lightning streaks across the back. "These don't work out here, you know. Out of tower range."

Fred examined his for a moment, and conceded that Prince Cale was correct. "Well, I'll have to make a land-line call then, to some of my friends, and see if we can get that fixed." He took a big sip of his latte, and sighed. "Always work to do."

"I've never worked a day in my life." Prince Cale stated, as if it were an accomplishment.

"I'm sorry," Fred stated. "I might be able to find you something to do, if you decided you're interested. But, we digress, what of this Hole in the Wall, and where is it actually. You say you were attacked by the wizard's evil minions?"

"Yes," Prince Cale moaned, as if just remembering the scratches on his feet, "there were many of them. And after a long walk down the beach, having my feet attacked was too much to bear. I saw her." He paused significantly, and looked towards the window. "She was a vision of loveliness, singing at the edge of the shore, with her feet just touching the waves." He sighed, and then stared into his cup of java. "Then her captor called for her, and she left, and the waves returned to cover the hole in the wall, so she cannot be reached."

"What about by boat?" Fred asked.

"The rocks would be too treacherous."

"Hmm." Fred wasn't sure he believe Prince Cale's tale, especially the part about the evil minions, and the hole in the wall. What wall? he wondered. He liked hiking down the beach, but thought he might wait for a better day, with less rain. "Thank you for telling me of your adventure. May I ask how you escaped?"

"Only by climbing back over the rocks to shore, as quickly as possible, to escape the returning waves called by the evil sorcerer."

"You live on the beach in the southlands?"

"Yes."

"Are you sure the tide didn't just return on its own, while you were out there?"

"Are you calling me a liar?" Prince Cale rose from his chair, offended, and grabbed at something in his pocket. He brought out a pen. "I'll sue you for slander."

"My apologies, Prince Cale," Fred used a soothing tone of voice, "I didn't mean anything of the sort." He waved towards a new barista, presumably Cassie, who had just taken her place by the espresso stand. "I'll buy you your next java, to make amends, if that is acceptable to you?"

"Oh, well," Prince Cale seemed mollified. "I suppose that would do."

Cassie approached, her hair hanging halfway over her face, "Yes, do you need something?" she asked in a throaty voice.

"Prince Cale needs a new drink, and I would like to inquire about an inn. Is there one nearby where I can stay for a night? I have some research I would like to conduct."

"The Rockaway Cottage may have space available, sir. It's just down the road a few blocks," she stated politely. Then she half-turned to Prince Cale, "and what would you like, sir?"

"Oh, well, I suppose a non-fat latte with an extra shot, and some almond flavoring would do nicely," Prince Cale stated. "Did the others tell you of my adventure this morning?"

"Why, no, sir." She stated somewhat disinterestedly.

"Well, I walked down the beach to the Hole in the Wall, following the voice of a beautiful maiden, a Princess held captive by an evil wizard who has evil minions at his beck and call," Prince Cale stated boldly.

"Really, sir? Well, I've been down that stretch of beach before, but I haven't encountered any evil minions." She covered her mouth with one hand. "However, I suppose, they may only attack young princes."

Fred noticed that she seemed amused, and wondered if she was hiding a smile behind her hand. It was hard to see her features with all of her wavy hair hanging over her face. Prince Cale seemed oblivious to her behavior, and nodded vigorously. "The wizard must be keeping all the Princes away on purpose to keep the Princess his captive. He probably has a spell to tell him when any Princes are around." He looked at Fred. "There are spells like that, aren't there?"

Fred battled within himself, not sure how he should answer. "I suppose some of the satellite technology could be used to screen unwanted visitors, or a good camera security network."

"Exactly," Prince Cale stated.

"Well, I'm glad you've got it figured out, gentlemen. I'll get your drink order now," she stated, and walked away.

Prince Cale looked surprised, and somewhat stunned, as if he wasn't sure exactly what had just happened. "You know, Prince Fred, I don't think this place is friendly to our kind."

Fred cleared his throat in an effort not to smile. "What do you mean exactly, Prince Cale?"

"When I came here, the ladies seemed appreciative of my role, and now . . . well, they seem to not realize who I am. It's as if I were just . . . anyone." Prince Cale looked aghast at his own words. He put his used cup down, and stood up. "Well, I think I should take my business elsewhere," he stated loudly.

"What about your latte?" Fred asked.

Cale looked serious for a moment, and then turned toward the espresso bar. "Make my drink to go."

"Of course, sir," Cassie stated. As she finished his drink she placed it on the espresso bar, for him to pick up.

Cale looked at the drink, and then at Fred. "Can you believe that? She didn't even bring it to me."

"I think that's the normal service that's offered," Fred stated. Since Cale didn't seem capable of getting his own drink off the bar, Fred walked over and picked it up. As he did so, he glanced over the espresso machine, and into Cassie's beautiful brown eyes. Perfect eyes, except for the frame of scar tissue around the one that had been covered by her hair earlier.

Her face tightened, as if expecting him to make some negative remark.

"Thank you, miss," Fred said, in his warmest voice. "Has anyone ever told you that you have perfect brown eyes."

"Don't mock me, sir. Prince or not, I'll kick you out of this establishment." Her voice came out hard and flat, and she stood stiffly.

"I wasn't mocking you, my lady. You do have beautiful brown eyes, and the other," he gestured towards her scar tissue, "really doesn't take away from them at all."

"Just leave," she said, and looked away, "please."

"I apologize," he said, and then he turned and walked

over to Prince Cale, handed him his drink, and opened the door.

Prince Cale seemed to think that Fred was opening the door for him, and he shouldered his way past Fred into the constant drizzle outdoors. "I think I'll join you at that inn. They must have something for men of our stations."

Fred wondered if his politeness had gotten him into trouble again. He really didn't want to hang around Prince Cale any longer, but he did sort of pity the fellow.

After a short ride on his motorcycle down to the inn, with Prince Cale reluctantly riding behind him, obviously terrified, Fred found their accommodations to be acceptable, clean and dry, each with his own private room. He discovered that Cale felt the rooms were beneath his station, and didn't want to pay. Fred suspected the Prince was short on money, and he footed the bill for Prince Cale's room, making sure the inn staff understood that it was for one night only.

The next morning dawned bright and clear. Prince Cale didn't answer to his knock, so Fred grabbed a continental breakfast, and inquired about the Hole in the Wall.

The owner of the inn, a wizened old woman, winked at him and said, "Ah, a quest? I might have known." She then leaned forward on the counter, and beckoned him to come closer.

Fred obliged her, and munched on a blueberry muffin while she spoke.

"Just down the beach you'll find,
A hole in rock, covered in slime,
As the tide washes out,
Be sharp and look about,
For a maiden fair
And a wizard's snare."

She stopped and gazed at him measuringly. "I think you'll do better than that other Prince. However . . . if you wish to succeed in your quest, you'll have to watch the tide. If you get stuck on the other side, pardon the rhyme, you might get stuck there for a few weeks."

"The wizard's spell?"

"No, no, it's right here in the tide tables," she said as she pulled out a small book labeled, "Tide Tables." "There won't be another slack tide low enough for passage through the rock unless you fancy making it passed the wizard and doing a little mountain climbing."

"I'll keep that in mind. Thanks for your kindness and

advice." Fred paused, wiping his face with a napkin, and then pulled out a business card. "If Prince Cale wakes and wants to look for work, just have him call this number. They'll help him out."

"Him, work?"

"Stranger things have happened."

"Hmph." She took the card and placed in room 212's box, and then busied herself at her desk.

Fred shrugged, and started to walk out. "Actually, if I do get stuck, will you keep my motorcycle in your garage?"

"If that happens, I'll charge it to your card, same amount as a room."

"That's steep."

"Most travelers bring their cars and need the space."

"All right." Fred accepted her price, and walked out the door with his pack slung over his shoulder. After a half hour of steady walking, he had to clamber over a log-swollen stream. Only a few minutes after that, he could see it. A perfect circle in the rock, with the waves crashing all around it framed the blue sky beyond. He realized that he should have asked the innkeeper when the tide would be out. As he walked closer, he realized the tide was receding, and his own respect for Prince Cale diminished even further. This wasn't a challenging walk. Sure, the sand caused a bit more work, but it wasn't even a two hour hike.

Satisfied that his motorbike would be safe, he started the long walk down the beach the direction that the innkeeper and Prince Cale had pointed out.

Since the tide still crashed around some steep rocks at the base of the hole in the wall, and it still appeared to be receding, Fred nestled himself against a large beached tree, and pulled out a small snack of trail mix. He didn't eat much, and as he waited he gazed out at the shore. With a sigh, he took in the awesome beauty. Waves crashed magnificently against rocks just offshore, and the shallows being revealed were full of tide pools.

Over the crashing waves, he began to hear a sound, a beautiful sound that begged his attention. A lovely, throaty voice, so low that he could barely hear it, issued forth from the Hole in the Wall. Fred gathered his pack, and stood up. Walking slowly over to the rocks, he could see that the ocean had receded more, with a shelf of rock extending from the shore towards the Hole in the Wall. The rock shelf looked slippery, and was slanted, but Fred wasn't sure when the tide would be slack. He would have to risk getting his boots wet, if he wanted to see this Princess who sang lovely songs on the other side of the Hole in the Wall. He didn't see any evil minions, but despite that Prince Cale's descriptions had been overblown, that didn't mean that he should let his guard down. He adjusted the knife sheath on his belt so it sat closer to his left hand, and he tightened the pack's straps.

Ready, he began the slippery walk on the rock shelf, cautiously avoiding the green and brown strands of kelp. He knew from other experiences that wet rock might look slippery, but kelp was slick and dangerous. He hated to step on barnacles, but he knew that these tough creatures could withstand an evenly place step, and they would grip the soles of his shoes. As he half-stepped, half climbed his way across the rock shelf, clinging to pieces of overhanging rock for balance, he noticed the amazing amount of life around him, especially in all the little holes in the rock, where puddles of seawater hosted sea snails, and sea slugs, barnacles, sea urchins and sea stars.

Watching both his step and the life below him, he realized as the wall he leaned against turned inward that he had reached his destination. The Hole-In-the-Wall was larger than he realized, opening up a whole new vista of rocky beach and sandy shore. A woman, with dark tresses, stood at the edge of one of the tide-pools. Her voice lilted and hummed, as she bent over the sea of life near her feet. The sound of it sent shivers into him, shivers of excitement and comfort at the same time. He felt warmed by her voice, and he knew that Cale had either not seen the same girl, or he had not described her well enough. Although her dark hair cascaded over her face, she had a beautiful figure, and long careful fingers that examined a sea snail, picking it up and then placing it back in the pool.

Fred stood there for a moment mesmerized by the sight and sound of her, and then he started walking toward her, not thinking of the kelp and rocks at his feet. He slipped slightly and put his hand out stupidly placing it against a barnacled rock. The sharp edges of the barnacles cut into his hand, but he waited until he got his balance before moving it upward, with no sideways motion. His care kept the cuts to pinpricks instead of gashes. As he studied the rocks by his feet more carefully, he picked his way through the tide pools until he reached the shore.

The singing had stopped, and he looked up to see the woman approaching him, her hair still swung forward in front of her face. Suddenly he realized who it was . . .

Cassie, the barista.

She must have recognized him as well, because she stopped, and flicked her hair back over her shoulder. "What are you doing here?"

"Prince Cale's tale . . . well, I wanted to see if it were true."

She laughed. "Well, do you see any evil minions of my father, the 'evil wizard'?"

"No, actually I haven't."

"Then how do you explain the cuts on your hand?"

"Barnacles and my own foolishness."

"Honesty, how refreshing. I didn't think your kind had it in you."

"You mean the prince kind, or wizards, or just men?"

She looked at him for a moment. "Mainly princes, but sometimes just men, and only evil wizards."

"Speaking of wizards, who is it that keeps you here . . . I mean, who did Prince Cale think was an evil wizard?"

Cassie laughed. "Probably my dad, who has an underwater lab, as well as an aboveground lab built into the Cliffside." She pointed behind her at the cliff.

As Fred looked up to where she pointed, he noticed

first the glint of solar panels, then windows. "Clever." He looked out toward the ocean. There just a few hundred yards out, situated next to a rock, he spotted a wind generator. "Solar, wind, and . . . wave energy as well?"

"I guess there's more to you than just an empty crown."

"I'm actually in town to meet with Clarence, the Wizard of the 5th kind, Alternative Energy Sources. My appointment's for Monday, but I had a few extra days. I hope your father doesn't mind that I came early, or came to his lab instead of meeting him in town." He smiled and shrugged ruefully. "I guess my crown is a little emptier than I realized, not putting Prince Cale's story together with what I knew about Wizard Clarence. He studies marine biology with three adult daughters, and he uses alternative energy as a sideline." He recited the facts, and felt foolish. "Were the evil minions that Prince Cale mentioned the barnacles, and the sea stars?"

Cassie laughed. "Barnacles and sea stars as evil minions?"

"He said they were numerous, and they cut his feet, and had many arms . . . barnacles are sharp," he held out his hand, "and sea stars do have more than two arms."

She laughed again, throwing back her head. "Ooh, scary sea stars . . . that is so unbelievable, and yet, given what I saw of your Prince Cale . . . the only explanation."

"My Prince Cale? I just met him, and trust me, he's not my type."

"Don't get started on types," she stated flatly, drawing away from him.

Fred cleared his throat and looked back out to the sea. He knew when a subject was closed. "So, why did the woman at the inn give me that rhyme about the evil wizard, if he's really a Wizard who works with alternative energy sources."

"Father doesn't like to have his privacy disturbed. Everyone in town knows the truth, and keeps the rumor going." She shrugged. "I wish they would take out the part about the Princess though . . . I don't like fools thinking that I'm some kind of treasure to be found or rescued. But I think my sisters like it . . . so I guess they're happy at least."

"Your sisters?"

"We co-own the Java shop in town. Sally was the one

that Prince Cale saw yesterday. And Bridgette is interested in you." She gave him a sideways glance as she said this.

"Well, too bad for her that I have my eyes on someone else." He gazed at her, waiting to see if she would flirt back.

She looked at him a moment, disbelief showing in her eyes, and then turned away. "My father would probably like to meet you, early or not. I'll take you there in a moment. I have to gather my samples."

"Samples?" he asked as he followed her to the tide pool where she had been examining earlier.

"I'm continuing my father's research on sea stars and their ability to regenerate their limbs. It's part of my doctoral work." She gazed back into the tide pool, down at the life there, and then reached around the rocky side of the tide pool, and picked up a bucket, filled partway with sea-water and two sea stars who were missing pieces of their arms.

"I read somewhere that they actually can regenerate all their limbs, if need be, is that true?" he asked her, hoping that his knowledge impressed her and didn't make him look like an idiot.

She looked at him again, her brown eyes widened

slightly. "Again, you surprise me, Prince. Not many people know about the sea stars ability to heal themselves. And your information is accurate. The interesting thing is that even if part of their main body is cut off, they can still become whole, and it has been speculated that two half-stars could become two different whole sea stars with the same DNA."

"And how do you intend to continue research in this area?"

"What do you mean?"

"How far are you willing to take your studies? And what will you do with this information, once you have verified your conclusions?"

"I'm hoping that my studies will contribute to the medical science magic, so that we can encourage the healing process more fully in patients who have lost a limb, or who have been burned," she said. She put her hand to her eye for a moment. "I obviously have my personal reasons, as well," she said, somewhat stiffly.

Fred didn't know quite what to say, so he just gazed at her for a moment, and then at the sea stars. Their tiny feet under their arms fascinated him, but not as much as the girl beside him. "We all have personal reasons for pursuing our work," he said. "I was drawn here by a quest to end the tyranny of the Power Kingdom Conglomerate. Your father's use of alternative power fascinates me. You may not know what it's like to live under the ruling of someone who turns off your power at a whim, in the hopes of gaining more profit from people who have little to give."

She reached out and touched his arm for a moment. "I have heard of the situation in the midlands. My father will gladly help you," she said. Then she blushed and withdrew her hand. "I think I have enough samples. Let's go meet him."

HAIKU - ROBOT

lights switch on displays

after the science fair ends

a mind awakens

WAR, INCORPORATED
EXCERPT

The silent trip from her home to the spaceport unnerved Janice. She kept picturing her mom's tear-filled face in the window as the hover-van pulled away. The vision filled her with grief that tore at her insides, and made her want to vomit since she couldn't cry in front of the two agents. Stupid, stupid, stupid. Mom had signed her away to the Federation, and she should be angry at mom's last minute emotional outburst. Knowing her mom's usual closed way of handling things, those tears couldn't have been real. But she wanted to believe that her mom might feel the same loss, and fear she was feeling. It didn't make enough sense, like some kind of crazy nightmare. She just wanted to wake up, and not feel the confused tearing of her heart and soul.

Outside the tinted windows, the horizon rolled by steadily, until they entered the security gates of the spaceport. There, the guards were disinterested in the van's occupants. Janice knew if she cried out for help, they would ignore her. No one wanted to interfere with UTF business. Entering an area of the spaceport that she had always wanted to sneak in and see, Janice found herself unable to focus on anything outside the van. The buildings were grey, lit up by huge lights that didn't cast any interesting shadows in the darkness. Implacable uniformity seemed to be the motto of the place, or maybe she just couldn't get a grip on anything while drowning in her own hurts.

The hover-van slowly glided to a stop, and then lowered slowly to the ground, as the agents set the controls for secure lock-up. One of the two twin agents opened Janice's side door, and waited for her. Janice didn't want to get out any more than she had wanted to get in, but she knew she had no choice. If she didn't move, the agent would move her. Unbuckling slowly, she stood up, and exited the van, feeling as if the world swayed under her feet. Hover-vans were known to have that effect on people, but Janice felt that it was only a reflection of how she felt inside. The waves of emotional turmoil matched her lack of balance. The agent eyed her for a moment, and then was joined by the other one. They looked at each other, and a silent communication seemed to pass between them, as if they could read each other's thoughts. Janice wondered if all clones acted like these two did, or maybe just UTF agents. She planted her feet shoulder width apart and took a couple of deep breaths. She wouldn't fall flat on her face in front of them, wouldn't give them any reason to touch her.

The one who had opened her door nodded at her, as if she had passed some small test, and then gestured to a small door ahead of them. "The processing unit is ready."

As he walked away from her, Janice followed, fighting a shiver that crept up her arms. A processing unit, whatever it was, didn't sound pleasant. And the other agent was following her. She could hear the squeak of his shoes, matching his partner's steps.

Inside the building, the first agent indicated that Janice should take the chair in the center of the room they had entered. On the opposite side of the room, another windowless door with an access code pad beckoned her. She wanted more than ever in this small room to get away from these two men, afraid of their strangeness, the physical wrongness that emanated from them. Hearing the click of the door shutting behind her, she knew that everything that happened after this was beyond her control. But still, she wanted to face down the terror of the unknown. When the second agent turned to face her, she tried to hold herself as tall as she could.

"You may remain standing if you so choose, but the process will take some time. Your kind does not have the stamina of genetic perfection."

Janice swallowed back an angry retort about the percentage of mutations in clones, and then put her hands on the back of the chair and waited.

"Have it your way." The first agent exited the small room through the inner door, and the second followed him. She could hear the beeping of a numeric lock setting, and then the lights in the room dimmed. Sweat broke out all over her body, and Janice fought the urge to crouch behind the chair for protection. Did mom know this kind of thing would happen to her? Would she have given her to these men, knowing about processing units? Janice sighed and shook her head to get out of the self-pity she felt, and then the humming of voices started.

Quiet at first, the sound of several voices speaking in different languages grew louder and louder, none of them making sense to her. It came from everywhere around her, and when Janice couldn't stand the noise, pressing her hands against her ears didn't block it out enough. She crouched lower and lower, until finally she was on the floor behind the chair, curled into a little ball. The voices just kept rising, and rising, seeming to grow faster and circle her.

With her head spinning from overwhelming dizziness, Janice started to cry. "Stop, please, stop. There has to be another way. Just stop it." The sound only increased, until finally Janice could see dark spots forming in front of her eyes. She shut them tightly, and then lost the contents of her stomach. The smell made her heave again and again, and she tried to squirm away from it. The scent followed her, just like the noise, and then a wall of blackness engulfed her.

Janice woke up with her arms underneath her, and her cheek pressed into a cold surface. Fear coursed through the inside of her arms, and she had to move, but she couldn't. The weight of sleep pressed her whole body downward. Even her eyelids were heavy, only allowing her to open them a crack.

Glaring white lights, and a blur of grayness caused her to close her eyes again. She wasn't home. She should be there. She took shorter, shallow breaths until a pain in her chest made her think. No, short breaths would make it worse. Long, easy breaths, just like her dad had always told her. She imagined his long dark hair falling over his face as he used to talk to her, try to calm her.

There, she was doing better now. That's what he would have said if he had been with her. She swallowed hard, and realized her mouth was dry, and her throat incredibly sore, like she was sick. She tried to move her head slowly, and the wave of dizziness she felt overwhelmed her. She put her cheek back on the metallic floor. There was a gentle hum she hadn't noticed before, vibrating through her cheek and into her jaw. It was almost pleasant. She decided to listen, and rest until she felt better.

How long she lay there, she didn't know. The humming gradually grew louder, and then there was a squealing sound like metal on metal. Janice was jolted up off the surface she was lying on, and came back down first on her knees, and then her hands, automatically catching herself before her head hit the floor. She was able to open her eyes now, and despite the brightness, she could see that she lay in a huge room full of kids, all sleeping on the floor, all life-wired. Looking at her own right arm, she saw that she was the same. Why hadn't she noticed before? And why was she awake?

She remembered the sounds that had deafened her to sleep, the pain of mom's rejection and betrayal that centered as always in her stomach. But when she awoke she had been thinking of her dad. She closed her eyes and felt caught by the red web of her eyelids. Red. Night terror. It came back now. Clones attacking her father and brother, red everywhere. She opened her eyes quickly, and bit her lips. She wasn't going to think about that anymore. Better to think about mom's silence, the look of anguish on her face before Janice left with the UTF agents. Janice hoped mom hurt inside as badly as she herself did, or worse.

The hum of the ventilation units in the metal walled and ceiling room grew louder. Warm air blew over her, and Janice settled back into more comfortable place on the floor. She should be getting up and investigating this place, she knew that. But something, the heat, maybe something in the lifewire made her drowsy. Without the memory of the night terror keeping her awake, Janice slept again. This time in her dreams, she heard her mom say the unthinkable words, I love you, over and over again.

Cold seeped into Janice's back, and she woke up

uncomfortably, wishing she could find some way to go back to sleep. Instead, with her eyelids cracked she could see the glare of lights overhead, and shut her eyes, willing herself to stay still.

She remembered . . . the voices . . . and then the images in the long silence. Images of insignias and rankings, weapons and movements, and then a strange nudge to return to her own dreams, and then the silence while she confronted her own mother, the ghosts of her brother and father, then back to the training in cultures, weapons, languages, combat techniques . . . until now.

Shuffling footsteps approached on her left side. "You're awake, don't try to hide it. The life-wire shows your bodily functions in an active state."

Janice squinted her eyes at a white-coated man standing above her, and looking at a handheld monitor. She clenched her hands together under the thin blanket, and then tried to relax.

The med-tech, that's what he was according to the symbols on his jacket, gave her a cursory glance, and then re-focused on the monitor. Med-tech, third class, that's what those stripes meant the dreams told her, and she accepted it, and then rejected it a moment later. How had she known? Was that what that awful processing was about?

The med-tech took the life-wire out of her arm with a quick yank, and pasted a small band over arm. "Well, sit up now, and when you feel steady, stand and take your place on the orange line behind you."

Janice turned away from him onto her side, realizing that she was clothed only in a thin shift, and her own body felt strange to her.

The med-tech took her reaction to mean that she wasn't ready, and touched her shoulder. "It's all right, it takes some time to adjust after four years of cold sleep."

Four years of dreaming sleep, four years lost. She wanted to clutch the blanket to her somewhat larger breasts but it would be a sign of weakness. She could almost hear mom's voice telling her that. But mom had given her up, and she didn't have to listen to that stern tone that replayed itself in her head. She bit her lips and looked around. Across the room, she could see a line of kids about her size, all standing at attention in front of a fat, balding officer. Between herself and them, hundreds of other kids lay asleep, some strapped to the narrow cots they lay on.

Janice pushed herself off the cot and the chill of the metal floor made her stand up straight. She would prove herself as one of them, even if it meant listening to the hated advice mom had given her.

They were mostly boys, and a with another jolt of surprise, she recognized one of them. Tonney, with his sneering grin, gave her a look of superiority. She sidestepped quickly, and kept moving.

"You could just ruin my life back home, you had to come here too."

Janice felt a flush of anger course through her, and her shoulders tensed up as she took a place at the right end of the line, three kids down from Tonney.

"What's that, crudet?" The portly officer, Lieutenant by his stripes, leaned into Tonney's face. Janice smiled to herself. At least no one liked Tonney any better here than they had at home.

"Nothing." Tonney's throaty chuckle made Janice flinch.

"Excuse me, collie?"

"Nothing, sir." Tonney's face smoothed into a serious expression.

"That's right, you're nothing. None of you collie brats amount to anything, and the money and time wasted on your training is ridiculous. You're all just going to be fodder for enemy fire."

"I thought that's why clones were invented, sir." A blonde girl spoke from down the line.

"Well, some will be used that way, but it turns out making clones isn't cheap, and your training, half-baked though it is, is cheaper. No one wants you."

Janice looked up at the crossbeams in the open ceiling that were dark and bare between the glaring lights. She didn't think any of them needed to be reminded of not being wanted. A heavy boot stamp in front of her brought her eyes forward, and with a shock she realized that the Lieutenant was shorter than her.

"Toes to the line, crudet and get your nose out of the air.

"Yes, sir." Janice hated the old pig already, just for making her stand out from the group.

"At least you crudets should be able to get the 'sir' part right, the computer should have scrambled your brains for that anyway." The Lieutenant turned away from her and looked at the others. "Remember that I am to be called 'sir' or 'Lieutenant Sagat'. Anyway who forgets the protocol of your sleep-training will get laps."

"Yes, sir." The chorus around Janice was weak, but Lieutenant Sagat accepted it. He gave her another glare before marching off down the line to another group joining them, and Janice sighed in some relief. As long as she kept Tonney as far from her as possible she might survive this horrible place.

The chance to observe the other cadets waking up gave her some insight into Lieutenant Sagat's attitude. Everyone was treated with callous casualness. He acted like he despised all of them, all of them being 'collies' and 'adopted contracts'. Out of the four hundred or so other cadets, there were only about fifty girls including her. At least the Lieutenant didn't treat them any differently than the boys. Janice had the last place on her end of the line.

Lieutenant Sagat came down the line, and stopped in front of her. Speaking loudly so that his voice boomed in the shipping bay, Sagat addressed her. "You, girl, give me your best salute."

She nodded, and snapped her hand towards her head, thumb under, and then brought it down to her stomach palm up. The motion seemed to come from some unconscious part of her. Her muscles seemed to know the move, even though she didn't think she had ever done it before. The fact rocked her back on her heels and she paused at the end of the salute. It was one thing for her mind to respond to the dreams, the computer's scrambling as Sagat referred to it, but to have her body react added another more frightening dimension to the four years in cold sleep.

Lieutenant Sagat leaned towards her, and pinched the skin under chin. It didn't hurt badly at first, but the pain increased the longer he held it. She finally realized what he wanted. "Yes, sir."

"Better, no nodding." The Lieutenant released her and walked back down the line. "Now, all of you, the salute."

"Yes, sir." Janice shouted out the response with the others, and they all snapped the salute. This time she expected the feeling of the salute when she tensed her arm, and twisted her wrist at the end. Mind and body working together, just like some of the dreams had taught her.

It went on like that. A waking dream of the things she had learned in cold sleep: the march, the insignias on the officers, and then came the gap.

When Sagat ordered her to lead troops to the barracks,

she stopped cold and just stared blankly at him. She ran the word barracks through her mind, but there was no sense of direction that came in response, no knowledge.

"Won't take leadership, is that it?"

"But I don't know, sir." Janice looked at the other cadets to see them staring past her.

"Don't know?" Lieutenant Sagat laughed in a short bark. "Don't give me that. I won't put up with insubordinate nonsense." He grabbed her arm, and shoved her against the wall.

Janice threw out her arms to stop her impact, and felt as if the world had dropped out beneath her once again. She should have known that physical punishment would take place here. The conditioning she had received hadn't been gentle. A part of her cried out at her mom's betrayal once again, but at the same time she balled her fists and turned to face Lieutenant Sagat. "Sir, the computer must have missed me in station schematics, because I honestly don't know it, sir."

He pinched the skin on her arm and rolled it around in his fingers. Janice gritted her teeth and tried not to wince. He pinched harder.

"Think you're tough, is that it, crudet?"

"No, sir." Janice wished Sagat would focus his attention on someone else, at least for a moment. If Tonney hadn't picked on her in the first place, none of this would be happening.

Lieutenant Sagat leaned closer to her, and she could smell the grease on his breath. "You could have made it through basic as captain of your team, but now you don't have a chance of survival." He released her and turned back to the others, focusing in on Tonney. "You, boy, take the troops to the barracks and choose a team for yourself for barracks 12A."

"Can't, sir. It's like she says, not there."

Janice looked away as Tonney smirked in her direction, and was sure that the Lieutenant was going to shove her into the wall again.

Instead, all she heard was a snorted laugh. "Like she says, hunh. Anyone else care to join these two in insubordination?" Lieutenant Sagat eyed them all angrily, and then shouted. "Volunteers to lead team to the barracks step up."

No one stepped out of their line, and the blow Janice

had been expecting earlier came. The Lieutenant's meaty fist knocked her sideways onto the ground but she caught herself rolling into the movement, just like she had been trained to do. She came up on the balls of her feet, back into a salute. "Sir." She hoped that by addressing him correctly, he would back off. Instead, he leaned in close to her, and started yelling.

"You think you're some kind of leader, cadet! Then you can lead your team around this shipping bay until you're ready to take an order. All of you, fall out!"

"Yes, sir." Janice started running around the outer rim of the shipping bay, hearing the others fall in behind her. She tried to keep an easy pace, but she couldn't be sure if everyone would keep up. She hoped they didn't all hate her.

A boy edged up next to her. He had the braids and coloring of a Bel-arrivan, a planet known for its ability to stand outside the UTF, and for the Bel-arrivan's rejection of cultural blending. What would a boy from a rich planet be doing among the adopted contracts? Maybe his mom didn't want him either. Janice allowed the tears to well up in her eyes, but then the boy nudged her, and winked.

"Nice shiner, I've been watching the others. The old

goat will figure out that we're not insubordinate soon enough. At least, not insubordinate on purpose, this time." He winked again, and fell in behind her as they neared the Lieutenant

The ugly man had crossed his arms, and widened his stance, as if ready for a long wait. He spit on the floor as she passed, and Janice winced reflexively away from him.

She wouldn't allow him to touch her again That thought came unexpectedly, and she knew that somehow, more than just the station schematics had been missed in her sleep-training.

CAPTAIN WRATH GOES CAMPING

Lightning flashed. Captain Wrath, aka Douglas Cranton, cursed loudly to satisfy his paying passengers, and then stumped over to his tent. Galaxy Cruise Lines had decided in their universal wisdom to add an overnight excursion to the Western Edge tours. In addition to the garish costume, foul makeup and other discomforts lavished on Douglas by his employers, the whole Smuggler's Cove Excursion on the newly synthed Looter's Island had nearly forced Doug to break his employee contract.

Thankfully, Doug had wrangled a few perks out of management, like his Captain's tent placed on the best campsite under a large canopy tree. In rotten weather like this, he could slip into the large tent and hope that the company didn't spring any surprise excursion adventures upon him.

A shrill scream interrupted his momentary hope.

Swearing again, he drew his pistol-blasters and threw

open the tent flap. The lanterns in the camp were all out, and only the wind driven rain greeted him. With the moon hidden behind the thick clouds, he couldn't see anything.

Doug stepped away from his tent, not wanting the light to make him a target. In the shadows of the canopy tree, he listened carefully for sounds of his crew. A silky murmur emanated from the tree behind him, and slender hands ran down his back.

"What the devil!" Doug shouted, jumping away from the hands.

A beautiful Dryadarian barely covered in brown bark smiled seductively at him. "Don't you want to have a little fun, Captain Wrath? Your passengers are all taken care of -

With a flick of his thumb, Doug changed the cartridge in his pistol, and shot her with universal sleeping gas.

She crumpled to the ground, and he stepped into the dense foliage.

Time to rescue his passengers again.

EMBERS

The wind is gone,
the trees are still,
clouds cover the sun,
my heart feels a chill.

But the embers glow
and from this I know
the spark still lives
and with each breath gives:

life to faith,
hope to love,
light to paths,
flight to me,

a phoenix rising.

ADRIFT

I close my eyes and I see light
The sun beats down burning bright,
The sands of time around me shift
And in that moment I am adrift
Caught by an eddy of space
Fascination of an alien race
They toil with such labor, on their
teeming ant hill, that they called earth.
A funny name, really, but it fits
A pile of rocks, earth, and sticks
That they pile up in something called "cities."
I call to the denizens of the deep.
They answer my call with a cry,
And I take them up with a sigh,
Relocating them to a planet more fair,
A place they can have a breath of fresh air.
Then I awake, and the dream fades,
I must really find some shade.

RUBY RED

Looking forward to a girl's night out with my best friends, I entered Once, the hottest club in town, with Sheila on my right and Holly on my left. We were arm in arm and laughing. A scene at the bar however, stopped me in my tracks.

"Hey Ruby, you made me trip," Holly complained.

"Are you all right?" Sheila asked, looking at me. "You look like you've seen a ghost," she said.

I took a deep breath, and started walking again. "No, I just . . . see a scene I don't like." I nodded towards the bar, and then veered to the left and found an open table.

Holly followed me, plopped down into the seat next to me, and looked towards the bar. "I don't see anything that exciting up there . . . except maybe that hunky guy hitting on a girl half his age," she said.

Sheila waved her hand for one of the waiters, and took another seat at the table, angling her chair to look up at the bar. "He's leaning in too close for her comfort, isn't he?" she commented.

"Men can be like wolves sometimes," I said, fingering the charm bracelet on my left wrist.

When the waiter came, he blocked my view, although with his good looks he could have been considered quite a view himself. I smiled at him, while he took my friend's drink orders.

"And for you, little lady?" he asked smiling.

My opinion of him plummeted. "I'll have a bottomless supply of caffeinated soda," I stated flatly. I may be small, but I don't like hearing about it.

"Coming right up," the waiter stated professionally.

"Oh, Ruby, why did you have to do that?" Sheila asked.

"What?" I asked in a mock innocent voice.

"She doesn't like being called little," Holly stated. "I don't like it when people call me big, or tall, or . . . moose," she muttered, frowning.

Sheila glared at both of us, and stuck out her lower lip. "If you two don't stop taking yourselves too seriously, I'll just find some cute guy to take me home."

I laughed. "I thought that was your plan originally," I said.

She smiled. "It always is . . . but I can never find one

that is brave enough to stand up to the two of you."

Holly tapped her hand on the table. "Just think of how many times we've saved you from Mr. Wrong," she said.

"Speaking of which," I said, getting up out of my chair, "it looks like our services might be required at the bar." I had been watching the wolfish guy keep leaning on the young girl, and I felt I had to do something. I wondered where that girl's friends were hiding.

Holly put her hand on my arm. "You never know, she might like to play hard to get."

I watched as he pulled his prey out of her chair and yanked her towards a back door. "I don't like it."

"I think I have to agree with Ruby on this one, Holly. That didn't look good." Sheila stood up, and patted me on the shoulder. "This time I get to help. You go do what you do, and I'll get the bouncer."

"All right," Sheila sighed. "I'll save our table."

"Thanks," I said, nodding to both of them. I swiftly followed the wolf-guy and his prey towards the back door, weaving in and out of the jostling crowd.

When I reached them the wolf-guy had the door open, and was struggling with his prey, who had just started to resist him.

"I thought you just wanted to talk someplace quiet," she protested.

"My car is real quiet," he said, holding her firmly in his grip with one hand. With his other hand holding the door open, he started dragging her outside.

I reached out and put a restraining hand on his wrist, right above where he gripped her arm. "I don't think she wants to go with you," I said. I looked at her pale face and slightly mussed hair and asked, "am I right, Miss?"

"I don't want to go to his car. I just thought he wanted to talk," she said.

"Come on, enough of this," the wolf-guy said. He turned and grabbed her with both hands, pulling her against his body.

Her eyes widened as he started dragging her toward the door again. "Please," she mouthed at me.

I really wished she would help herself out a little more, but I remembered being young and foolish myself. So I stepped forward on my left foot, and kicked him in the back of the knee with my right as hard as I could.

He stumbled, let her go, and turned on me. "You little

—

"Don't call me little anything," I growled.

"Excuse me, ladies," a deep voice interrupted.

I turned slightly to see Steven, the huge, muscular bouncer for this club standing next to me.

"Is this man bothering you?" he asked.

"Yes," I said.

"Bunch of baloney, I just wanted to take my girl out and have quiet talk, when this pushy little broad kicked me," the wolf-guy accused.

"He was dragging her towards the door, and I thought I should stop him," I stated simply.

Steven looked at me sternly. "It's my job to handle things like this."

"Yes, it is." I stated, putting one hand on my hip, and then gesturing with my right hand.

"You, sir, need to vacate these premises," Steven said harshly to the wolf-guy. He pointed to the exit.

Amazingly, the predator left, although he snarled at me under his breath.

I pretended not to hear him, and smoothed down my bright red mini skirt.

"Thanks so much," the girl said. "I didn't realize he was going to be so aggressive."

"Where are your friends?" I asked her.

"Oh, they ditched me," she said.

"You could sit with my friends and me," I said, pointing back to my table where Holly and Sheila sat. "We're just hanging out."

"Well, ok," she said shyly, twisting her hair in her hands.

Steven nodded, and said, "Good. Ruby will take care of you, and she might even tell you a little story."

I rolled my eyes at him, "Steven, you so wish you hadn't mentioned that."

"You know each other?" the girl asked.

"Yes, I come here too often," I said.

"I keep hoping there's a reason," Steven stated, winking at me, "other than helping me kick the riff-raff out."

"I'm Ruby," I said, ignoring Steven, "and when I was little, people used to call me 'little Red.'"

"Like the story, Little Red Riding Hood?" she asked.

"Yes, like the story," I said, fingering my charm

bracelet again, finding the charm I'd had since I was a little girl. It was a red cloak, just like the one my Grandmother made for me so long ago.

CHAMELEONS

Chaz heard a creak in the darkness behind him in the direction of the hallway and he immediately set the mainframe detonator. His checklist of sabotage was finally complete.

The door behind him crashed open, and Chaz jumped onto the table, changing in mid-leap into an ape. With legs made for leaping, he catapulted himself up toward the window ledge above him, and just in time. He felt the air behind him move; felt the near-touch of his would be captors. He turned to see who it was, and his eyes adjusted in the darkness to see – a tiger.

His shock nearly undid him, but as the tiger sprang for him, he reacted quickly, slipping out of the window and leaping into the air, again changing – but this time into a bat. He flapped his wings madly for a moment, and then glided away into the dark shadow of the building.

Once in a secluded corner, he changed again, this time into a cheetah. With quick strides he sprinted across the deserted parking lot and down the nearby street. He knew he wouldn't have much time to sprint in this form. He made it through the small town, and loped into the grassy sand dunes.

Knowing that pursuit could be right behind him, he continued to run until he splashed through the shallow waves. As his paws left the ground and he paddled into the water, he transformed back into his normal man shape, and stroked as powerfully as he could into the deeper water, diving under the waves, changing into a shark. He swam on as a shark for a while, and then as the water became deeper, and he left all vestiges of waves behind him, he changed again, lengthening and growing into a whale. As he surfaced to take in air, he heard an explosion behind him, almost deafening in this form. The waves of sound traveled through the water with intensity.

He continued to swim on, away from the shoreline, and out into the sea. As he swam, he reveled in the wonderfully cool water around him and this shape's ability to stay warm, as he swam purposefully away from danger. After several hours of hard swimming, Chaz hoped he had lost his pursuers, and changed his course, for another shore. He had been surprised by the presence of another shifter, but yet, he should have known. He felt a gnawing in his gut that went beyond his body's hunger, and knew that he hadn't acted swiftly enough on the information he had discovered a few months ago. The government wanted to make others like him. They weren't satisfied that he worked for them. They wanted to make their own shifters. So they had experimented with drugs, and genetics. He thought he had found the lab in time, before they had become successful, but he knew that had been no ordinary tiger behind him.

And they had caught him in the act. They would know it was Chaz that had sabotaged their labs, and destroyed their work.

Despite his body's weariness he had to keep on swimming hard toward the shoreline of his home. He had to make it there before they did. He had to save Cammie, his dear wife who had no idea that they were coming after him. They might take her to make him turn himself in, and then he would have to do as they wished. He couldn't allow them to harm her.

He turned his focus back to his swimming, the undulation of his huge body moving powerfully against the water, yet leaving very little ripples as he surfaced and dove. He loved this form. The first time he had become a whale, he had been on vacation with his parents, kayaking in the San Juans. Such heaven. The water was a constant source of comfort and information with so many scents, sounds and sensations surrounding him. He lost himself to the rhythm of the movement, and his form.

Hours later, he realized that he had begun to fall asleep, slowing in the water, and surfacing less often. He felt foggy, and definitely hungry. He tried to shift, but couldn't. However, the land wasn't far away. He pushed his body toward it with large undulations. He was almost there, but before he reached the shallow water, something bumped into his side and then he felt a searing pain. A shark had attacked him. He couldn't change forms, and the shark obviously sensed his weariness. He tried to circle around and take a bite out of the shark, but it reacted too quickly, darting away, and circling him.

With the small amount of energy he had left, he surged forward and beached himself.

He shifted back to his human self, hoping that he would be able to end up more on the sand than in the sea. As he shifted, the shark swam away confused.

Getting up, he stumbled to the sand, and fell with his feet still in the water, as the stabbing pain in his side grew worse. Blackness surrounded him, and his last thoughts were of Cammie. He hadn't wanted her to get hurt by all this.

He woke to the sound of voices, and the feeling of something, some cloth being wrapped around him, as he was rolled into it.

"Cammie?" It couldn't be her, but he wished it was. Blackness engulfed him again.

He woke to the softness of sheets and the warmth of blankets. He was in a room, with the smells of humanity and housecats surrounding him. He peered through the darkness and could make out a sewing machine on a table, with a basket next to it. The weight on his legs was a cat, whose green eyes glowed at him in the darkness. He moved his legs, and the cat moved haughtily away, jumping off the bed with a thump. His side still ached, but it was bandaged, and he felt groggy, as if someone had given him pain medicine.

There were voices, coming from beyond the door and moving closer. He struggled with the urge to shift to a different form and hide, and then forced himself to stay still. Whoever had helped him would be alarmed by not finding him as they had left him.

"Are you awake, in there?" A man's voice asked.

"Yes," Chaz said.

"I'll come in then," the man said, looming large in the doorframe. "Watch your eyes," he said, as he flipped a light switch.

Chaz squinted against the glare, and into the gentle face of an older man with graying hair. His piercing blue eyes looked at Chaz with some expectation, some eagerness that Chaz didn't understand.

"We found you on the beach. Saw you come in."

Chaz went completely still, barely breathing, wondering exactly what "they" had seen.

More footsteps came down the hallway, and an older woman appeared, her white waist length hair pulled back in a braid. "You were in your spirit form in the waves, and then took your human shape on the beach," she stated, looking at him with deference. "Our son took the form of a seal. Such gifts can come only from God." Then her eyes twinkled. "Of course, having ancestors from Ireland, and Iroquois also helps."

Chaz opened his mouth to deny any such heritage, or belief, but then he stopped himself. These people had helped him beyond common courtesy. Besides, the fact that they knew other shifters meant that they might know more than he did about people like him.

"You look thirsty, and I have coffee, and some breakfast cooked." The woman stated.

"Thank you," Chaz said. "I . . . am thankful for all your help." He sat up partway, ignoring the sharp pain in his side.

"You're welcome." The man said. "My name is Don, and my wife's name is Dawn." He smiled. "We make a great team, and we try to help folks that need help no matter where they are in life." He sat down on the bed. "You seem to be in trouble."

Chaz took a deep breath, not knowing what to say. "I am, and I can't repay you at all. I need to get going as quickly as possible."

"It's no problem. Look, I have some clothes that might fit you." Again, Don smiled, as if at the thought of Chaz filling out his clothes. "When you're dressed, come out to the kitchen for some coffee and breakfast, and we'll figure things out."

At a simple wooden breakfast table, Chaz dug into

fried potatoes and eggs, humming appreciatively at the spicy flavors that Dawn had mixed into them. He watched Don and Dawn out of the corner of his eyes, and liked what he saw there. They loved each other with every glance, and with every movement. It seemed like they were just halves to a perfect whole. He knew only a lifetime of loving looked like that and hoped that he could have that with Cammie someday.

When he was finishing up his coffee, Don spoke to him again. "We know that you must be anxious to be on your way, but before you go, we have to ask this . . . do you know of any others like you?"

Chaz stopped sipping his coffee and put his cup down, twisting it in his hands. "I didn't until yesterday." He paused, unsure of how to tell them of his foolishness. "I found out recently that some of my . . . 'business' associates were trying to make others like me."

They were silent, just watching him across the table, so he continued. "I went to their lab to destroy their work, but there was someone there with my . . . 'gift'." He gripped his cup hard. "I don't want you to get hurt for helping me, and I've already said too much."

"You've said enough." Dawn stated calmly. "We can take care of ourselves, and we have taken care of others who have walked the paths with us. We will give you enough to get you on your way."

"Thank you," Chaz said. He felt overwhelmed by their kindness, but he knew he had to be on his way to save Cammie.

After a few hours driving down the road in Don's old rusty loaner, he was only a few miles from home, and yet he felt weariness pulling at him. His wound took a great deal of energy to heal, especially when he wore a different form. However the benefit was that he would heal faster than any normal human, for as a shape shifter his cells were used to knitting themselves together in different ways as he willed them. Sometimes when Camille talked of her work as a nurse and a researcher in the field of medicine, he thought of telling her about his secret. His "gift" might be considered useful medically, but it was too risky. He didn't want to end up in a lab.

He yawned, and knew that he would have to take another rest before getting home. By now, the men after him might have traced his tracks to Camille, but if they had, he would not have the strength to confront them in his weakened condition.

Pulling off the highway, he found a side road, near a wildlife refuge. He had stopped here before to experiment changing his form. Now he welcomed the familiar road, the familiar parking lot, where he could park, and lean the seat back, allowing his form to change to its normal state. The fatigue was incredible, but it still took willpower to make himself rest, for Camille's sake.

When he awoke, he awoke with a start, and the knowledge that someone was near him. Someone female. He didn't open his eyes, but tried to look relaxed, shifting to his side, as if he were still asleep.

Rap, rap, rap-rap-rap! Someone, that same someone, was rapping at his window. It was no use to try and pretend to sleep as he tried to sort out her vaguely familiar scent. He sat up, and looked up, into sky-blue eyes, an oval face, framed by flaming red hair. The woman wore wildly colored clothes, which he noted were something like he expected a gypsy to wear. Her perfume confused her scent, and he couldn't make out what she actually smelled like underneath it, although again, he felt as though she were familiar, and he could trust her.

She waved at him through the window.

He unrolled it slightly. "Yes?"

"Hi," she said cheerily. "I was just wondering if I could hitch a ride from you?"

"Uh," his tired mind slowly came awake to wariness. Who was this woman and where had she come from? He took a quick glance around the deserted parking lot. "Where did you come from?"

"Oh, I was up early, with a lot on my mind, and I walked from town, it's only a few miles from here."

Chaz thought about that. It was possible that she had been out on a walk, and she was right about the distance. However, it still didn't seem right. "Where are you headed? Back to town?"

"Well, no, I thought it was about time for a road trip."

"Without a car?"

"Well," she smiled shyly, "the circumstances seemed to suggest that I needed to try a new venue. Do you know what I mean?"

"No," Chaz stated flatly, then he repented. For all that he knew she was exactly who she appeared to be, a young, footloose traveler. "Look, I don't mean to be rude, but I am in a bit of trouble and need to get into town quickly. If you want to go that direction I'll take you."

She shrugged. "Ok, I guess I could go back and pick up a few things." Then she smiled. "Plus, you sound as if you have an interesting story to tell."

"I can't tell it, but go ahead and get in." Chaz reached across the car, and unlocked the door. It was an ancient 70's model without any bells or whistles.

"So, what are you in a hurry for?" She asked as she slid in and closed the door.

"My wife."

"You're in trouble with her?"

"No." Chaz said, as he pulled off the road and headed into town. "Well, I don't think so, but I was supposed to be back yesterday."

"Why the road stop?"

"It would take too long to explain," Chaz said, not wanting to reveal his injury to her.

"And then you'd have to kill me?" She said this with a smile, obviously joking.

"No, but someone might," he said seriously.

Her eyes widened. "So you are in trouble, but not with

your wife . . . is she in trouble too?"

"I hope not."

"So you care about her a lot?"

Chaz glanced at her, annoyed by the question. "Yes, I care about her a lot, she is the love of my life, the one I want to grow old with."

"Oh, I didn't mean to be rude. It's just that I wondered if you were returning for her, or for something else, some memento or piece of information you needed." As she said this, her voice changed timbre slightly.

Alarm coursed through Chaz, and he slammed the brakes, swerving the car into the ditch. "Who are you?!" he demanded, turning to face her.

Her features melted, twisted, changed, and there, next to him, sat Cammie. Or someone who looked like her.

"Who are you?" he breathed quietly.

"Cammie, your wife, your love, just as you are my love, but I had to be sure of you."

"What do you mean, be sure of "me"?

"I had to make certain it was you . . . although you smell distinctly like you . . . and I had to make sure you were returning for me, and not something else."

Chaz could only stare at her, feeling undone . . . she had lied to him. Well, she hadn't told him the whole truth of herself, just like he hadn't told her. "How long have you known about me?

She looked away, her face tightening. "I knew we were going to get to that sooner or later, and I could lie, I suppose, because you do talk in your sleep . . . but we've had enough lying already between us." She looked back at him, and her face softened, and tears ran down her cheeks. "Chaz . . . I love you, but when I met you . . . you were a case study for me. They paid me to . . . . to . . . to watch you and study you. But I started falling in love with you the first day . . . and every day after that."

Chaz just looked at her, with hollowness inside of him that he hadn't felt in years. A hollow loneliness that gnawed at his guts. "You expect me to believe that?"

She closed her eyes and her face tightened again. "I know I deserve your suspicion, Chaz, but then you haven't been exactly forthcoming with me, as your wife, about your abilities, either."

"When are they going to be here?"

"What do you mean?"

"How long are you supposed to stall me so they can pick me up?"

She sighed, wiped away her tears, and gave him a challenging glare. "I left town because of you. I left all the research that I've worked on because of you. 'They' showed up at my door last night, and I gave them the slip around midnight. They don't know what I am any more than you did."

Chaz raised his eyebrows. He wanted to believe her, but he still thought it might be an elaborate set up. She had admitted to working for them, but then so had he. "You expect me to believe you?"

"I had hoped you would."

"Did you help them create others like us?"

"Others like us?" She frowned. "They used my research for that? Oh, I have been a fool." She balled her hands into fists. "It all makes too much sense. The questions they asked me . . ." she stopped and bowed her head. "I should have known. I was researching human genetics, and the possibilities that "shape-shifters" like us could aid modern medicine, heal people of diseases, wipe out cancer." She pounded her fists against her legs a few times. "The questions they asked . . . I should have seen where they were going . . . they could couple my research with cloning research and create shape-shifters."

"No." Chaz stated, both as a denial and as a hope. "The one I saw was fully grown, not a clone." Quickly, he described the lab to her, explaining that it looked like they had used some kind of change-agent on adult cells.

"Impossible."

"Improbable, and they probably killed many of their early test subjects before it worked. I thought I had discovered it in time to put a stop to it. Even if they had been doing research the entire time I've been working for them, it would only give them three years, and I doubt that's enough time to clone anything."

"No, the science . . . well, I just don't believe a change agent would work. I think you might have seen someone like us, someone working for them. They gave me another set of shape-shifter DNA to work with . . . they never told me where it was from." She fidgeted in her seat, and turned to face him. "Look, I love you, but I understand that you don't trust me right now. However, we could unravel this problem together. Work against them. Dispose of all their research and equipment. Drain their financial aid with the help of some well-timed losses."

"I want . . ." he began, and then the import of her words sunk in. "You were working for them, out of your lab here in Olympia?"

She nodded.

"I destroyed their mainframe, in Japan, and I sabotaged three other labs, but not one near here. I thought I had finished their work, but . . ." he ran his hands through his hair, feeling helpless against the enormity of the task before him. He felt so alone against a mountain of odds.

A familiar, comforting quote came to him, one that always calmed his fears . . . "You don't have a soul. You are a soul. You have a body."

He hadn't realized he had quoted it aloud, until Cammie whispered, "C.S. Lewis."

Somehow that answered and filled the hollowness inside of him. She understood. She could understand what he meant more than anyone ever could. With her help, they could find others like them, and they would have a chance against the odds that faced them. "I'm going to need help, if we are going to succeed, and I think I have an idea of where to get it." As he said this, he placed his hands on the well-worn steering wheel.

She put one of her hands over his. "I'm in, if you'll have me."

He took it and turned it over, feeling her pulse, smelling her particular scent, and knowing that somehow no matter what happened, he could trust her. He pulled her hand to his cheek and folded it around his face. "Always."

HAIKU – SPACE

Haiku – space #1

The final frontier
deadly planets, toxic to
Captain Kirk posers

Haiku – space #2

Starry horizon
beckoning us to come
play supernova

INTERROGATION

Doug woke in an instant, remembering the fight. Restraints on his wrists and ankles kept him from leaping out of his chair, but it toppled forward.

He hit knees first, and then forehead.

Husky laughter greeted him, and a pair of stiletto heels sauntered past his side view. "Get him up," said the familiar woman's voice.

A bulky figure hauled his chair upright and he faced the woman from the spaceport bar.

She leaned in close to him and whispered, "Now, Dougie, be a good boy and tell me why a cruise ship captain would be interested in my cargo."

Doug looked at the single light bulb hanging above her head.

She drew back, and placed her long fingernails against her cheek. "Whoever's paying you isn't paying you enough to go against us, trust me."

"No one's paying me," he said angrily.

"What? That's ridiculous." Her eyes narrowed. "Unless

you think you can make a profit from trafficking on your own . . .which you can't unless you have the right contacts." She dug her sharp nails into the side of his face. "Who are your contracts?"

Doug gasped, surprised by the pain. How in the world did this woman get her nails that sharp? He had to get out of here, but he couldn't see much of the room. He didn't think she had more than one bodyguard with her, because he hadn't heard anyone else.

"Who are your contracts?" she asked again, digging her nails in deeper.

Doug tried to ignore the pain.

"Pay attention, Doug. You don't know who you're dealing with here." As she spoke, her voice changed in pitch, and he could see the pupils of her eyes narrow to oval slits. Her cheekbones enlarged and fangs sprouted along her upper teeth.

Doug shuddered. Out of all the races from the Faerland Galaxy, those that could change form were the only ones that truly frightened him. "I don't need payment to free slaves," he said.

She drew back with a roar, her face morphing oddly

between the form of a woman and a cat.

Doug felt himself break into a shivering sweat, terrified.

Finally, she stopped, and said, "Tell me how you knew about the cargo, and you might not have to die."

"If I die today, I die knowing that I saved 300 people from the misery you intended." Doug tried to shrug nonchalantly. "Go ahead."

Suddenly, a huge crashing noise from behind Doug interrupted the interrogation. Weapons fire filled the air, and Doug threw himself to the side, knocking his chair over on purpose.

The woman changed the rest of the way into a tigress, but bullets cut her down in mid-leap.

Soft hands pulled untied Doug's hands, and Doug twisted to see Telli behind him.

"Good to see you alive, and whole, Captain Wrath."

"Good to be alive," Doug said.

"Let's not tell the crew that I had to save your hide this time, Captain, or your reputation will be ruined."

"Agreed."

CHAMPION IN THE DARKNESS EXCERPT

1 VISIONS

Lightning struck from the thick black clouds all around her. The burning man raised a fiery sword above his head and Clara cowered in the wet, slimy mud with a broken sword in her hands. Sharp, harsh sounds of fighting surrounded her, and the smell of smoke filled her lungs. When the dark lightning flashed again and the fiery sword began its descent, Clara's eyes flew open and she gasped for air.

The recurring nightmare had struck again. The lightning burned into the blackness of sleep was replaced by sunlight pouring into her room, hitting her directly in the face. She closed her eyes, and tried to remember the details. She felt like she had to replay it, had to understand it. The darkness had been filled with the noise of battle, but underneath that, there had been chanting voices. It didn't make sense.

Despite being covered in sweat from her nightmare, she shivered and goose bumps rose on her arms. Burrowing into her quilts, she curled into a ball on her side.

"Wake up, sleepyhead," sang out her father's baritone voice. "Rise and shine and give God the glory, glory."

Clara smiled under the covers, but groaned out loud. At fifteen, she didn't really want her dad singing songs to her in the morning, did she? Well, maybe a little, and his job as a Shepherd and teacher just seemed to pour out over in all aspects of his life. Shepherds led their flocks in prayer, study, and song, and her Dad's special love was music.

Clara opened her eyes and pulled the covers back just enough to see her Dad. His eyes twinkled. He had always been the morning person in the family, waking well before sunrise to start his prayers of thanksgiving and his study of the sacred scrolls.

"Am I raising a sword master, or a butterfly?" he asked, teasingly. "You keep wrapping yourself in a cocoon each night, so one of these mornings, I'll expect you to have wings."

"Dad," she groaned again, and frowned at him, "I'm not a little girl anymore. I know I'm not going to grow wings overnight."

His face stilled for a moment, looking almost sad. "Ah, but you have," he said. "You've grown up, and today your wings will take the form of a sword of power, the weapon of masters and senior apprentices."

He sat on the edge of her bed, and cupped her face in his soft hands. "You'll always be my little girl, even when you're off fighting and I won't be able to protect you." He leaned down and kissed her forehead. "May the Lord lift you up on wings like eagles, and keep you safe."

Clara wished her dad wouldn't be so melodramatic about her growing up, but she knew he meant well. If he hadn't been so serious already, she might have told him about the nightmares. As it was, she didn't want to concern him any further. She reached up and hugged him hard, squeezing him to let him know she wasn't going anywhere yet.

He held her against his lean frame for a few minutes, and then let her go. Standing up quickly, he brought a hand to his eyes, turning away from her. His voice came out husky, when he spoke. "Time for breakfast. Mom toasted some nut bread, and cut some papaya just for you."

"Thanks Dad," Clara said, trying to put reassurance in her voice. After he left, she changed quickly from her pajamas into loose fitting pants and a shirt. Both were gray, marking Clara as a sword apprentice. She stood in front of her small mirror to braid her shoulder length reddish blonde hair, and tried to frown at her reflection. It didn't work. The freckles across her upturned nose seemed to refuse to be serious for long. She wondered how many sword masters had freckles. It didn't seem fair, even if she did like a good prank now and then. Her lifelong passions included sword work, and studying the legends of sword masters. She couldn't imagine any of the Champions or heroes of the Triune Halls in ages past with freckles and an upturned nose. The pictures in the history texts made the Champions and heroes appear somber and determined.

Clara crept out of her room on her tiptoes, hoping to catch her mom unawares. They often tried to sneak up on each other, practicing sword scout skills with a bit of play. As she paused outside the threshold of the kitchen, she peered in carefully at her mother.

In their small kitchen, her mother was dressed in sword master black with the insignia of the Sword Guards on each shoulder. Her mom's straight blonde hair was pulled back in a tight braided bun, and she stood facing the window.

"Juice or tea for breakfast, Clara?" her mother asked, not turning from her work at the cutting board.

"Tea would be wonderful, mom," Clara said, slightly envious of the way her mother seemed to sense her presence even when she had been sure that she had been silent.

"Good, then why don't you get that, while I finish cutting the fruit," her mother said.

Clara found the tea and the tea pot, and quickly filled the earthenware pot with the hot water already steaming on their stovetop. Setting the tea pot on the small round table, Clara drew out three cups and placed them in their usual places. The small round table where they ate most of their meals only fitted up to four people, and Clara liked the coziness of it. She sat on the side that faced the open living area, her dad faced the open window, and her mom sat nearest the stove, always ready to jump up and stir something, if needed.

Everything felt so normal this morning, as her mother brought the fruit to the table, and her father reached out his hands to pray.

The words of the prayer tumbled over her head, in a

comforting cadence, but Clara was thinking about the day ahead of her, and tingling with excitement. She started bouncing her legs under the table.

"And please give Clara wisdom today in the Chamber of Choice, Lord. Amen." Her father finished praying and winked at her.

Clara stopped bouncing her legs, and winked back at him.

"You're ready for today, Clara," said her mother, covering one of Clara's hands with her calloused right hand. "I'm proud of you, and will always be."

"Thanks Mom," Clara said, smiling widely.

"Now, get some food into you, so you can keep your strength up," her mother said, pulling back her hand and picking up a thick slice of nut bread.

Clara did the same, thankful for the delicious food that warmed her and relaxed her. Her mom and dad shared a lot of duties around their small apartment home, in keeping with their busy schedules as Sword Guard and Shepherd Teacher. Clara helped them by keeping her own things picked up and clean, along with helping with the roof garden during the summer months.

After their breakfast, Clara went back to her room and put on all of her practice armor. A sword belt, boots, hard leather breastplate, wrist guards, a close fitting helmet, and a small pack with essential supplies all went on easily as they had every morning for the last seven years.

When she went to sheathe her sword, she paused for a moment, looking at her distorted reflection in its surface. Today she would replace her training blade with a sword of power, the weapon of Triune Hall Sword Masters. She would almost miss the training sword. It fit so well in her hand. She sheathed that blade one last time, and strapped her small round shield to her pack.

Back in the kitchen, her mother and father were washing up the breakfast dishes together in companionable silence, affectionately bumping into one another as they worked.

"I'm ready to go," Clara said.

They turned, her mother wiping her hands on the dish towel that her father held for drying. Her mother's blue eyes crinkled at the corners, and she smiled slightly. "You look like a young master already," she said. Then she crossed the small room in a few steps and folded Clara in her arms. "You'll always be my baby, but I'm so glad you've chosen the way of the sword, Clara. You can take care of yourself and your friends, and I don't have to fear for you."

Clara's dad laughed a short laugh. "Our baby's putting herself in the path of sharp edges, but you are less worried for her than if she chose a Shepherd's robe? You still amaze me, dearest."

Clara's mom squeezed Clara one more time, and then turned to her husband, her back slightly tense. "You know why, Farrald," she said quietly.

As always, Clara wanted to ask just what her mother meant by that remark, so like many other remarks made around their home that remained unexplained. Her mother had promised to tell her more about her past when Clara was old enough. She hoped that today might become that day, or after her inclusion in the circle of Sword Masters.

Farrald wrapped his arm around Juliay, and kissed the top of her head. He smiled at Clara. "You're going to be late if you dawdle with us, Clara." He came over and gave her a short hug, and then stepped back. "We'll see you at luncheon today, to celebrate."

"See you then," Clara said, and still smiling she left

their apartment, going down the outdoor steps past the music store below them.

The instruments hung silent at this hour since customers normally appeared just a few hours before luncheon and left a while after dinner. Clara glanced over the instruments as she passed, wondering which one she would play if she could. Her dad played the lute and the pipes. She enjoyed the music of the thrimble, a three stringed instrument with a thick neck and a short body. Then she put her hand on the leather wrapped hilt of her sword, the instrument she had chosen years ago as a child in the Desert district.

Clara followed the shortest route to the Triune Halls, hardly noticing anything around her, thinking over all the choices she had made that led to today's choice, the entrance into the Crystal Sword chamber. As long as she could remember, she had tried sword fighting with sticks. When Master Stelia had come to the Triune Halls of the Desert district, Clara had wanted to follow the mysterious, foreign swordswoman everywhere she went. When the Triune Council decided they needed her parents' skills in Skycliff, the capital city of Septily, she had told them formally that she wished to enter training as a Sword

Master. At eight, she had been the second youngest apprentice. Her friend, Salene, had been the next youngest. So many days of training had led to this day.

She wondered what kind of sword she would choose. She had thought about it many times before, but still didn't know.

She felt a swirl of excitement as she thought through all the colors of crystal swords available: yellows, browns, blues, purples, greens, reds, oranges, and even blacks. She knew each had meaning, and each matched the temperament and soul of the master that carried them. Her mother carried a dark navy sword with hints of purple in its depths, which stood for determination and nobility.

Suddenly, a hand blocked her vision, and she stopped, blinking, at her friend Salene. With a silly grin on her face, Salene didn't look like the daughter of an out of favor noble. Her short dark hair framed her narrow face, and she looked physically stronger than any of the noblewomen who fluttered around the dress shops. Her dark eyes twinkled with merriment.

"Are you sure you're ready for today with your head in the clouds?" Salene teased, waving her hand back and forth in front of Clara.

Clara batted her hand away, and stuck her tongue out at her friend. "I'm ready enough," she said. "The Sword Council grilled me for an hour yesterday, even after the Sword Teacher's board examined me."

"I know," Salene said softly. She put her arm through Clara's and tugged her down the street. "But you're ready, so let's get you there, and get it done, even if that means I'll be missing you after that."

"I won't be leaving for my practical internship for at least six months," Clara said, then she waved at Mr. Balent, their friendly neighborhood baker.

He waved and threw them both warm rolls that they caught easily. Clara started munching hers right away, but Salene tucked hers into her satchel.

"Yes, but you'll be busy with your duties," said Salene, echoing Clara's dad's worries. "And when you go, you have to visit each of the seven halls from the seven districts of Septily," she said. "That's going to take a while, and I'm going to miss beating you at footraces."

"Miss beating me, or getting beaten?" Clara asked, jostling Salene to the side of the street.

Salene disentangled herself from Clara's arm, gave her

a playful shove back, and said, "Beat me to the Hall gate, then, Master Swordswoman." She took off at a sprint down the street.

Clara dug her toes into the hard cobblestones beneath her, and ran after her friend, throwing everything she had into the moment.

Ahead of her, Salene navigated her way between early morning vendors who were attempting to set up their sales wagons on the street sides.

Clara scrambled after her, barely missing a bird seller, and forced to jump over a basket of eggs. Angry shouts followed her, but she kept running hard.

Salene took a right turn early, and they sprinted down an open alleyway and onto the Palace Way. This early, there were no courtiers about, only two of the King's mysterious Shadow Guards at the gate. Salene and Clara looked at each other, and pushed themselves harder.

At the intersection of Palace Way, and Hall Road, Clara stretched past Salene, managing to stay a hand ahead of her until they reached the cherry tree at the outer walk. Breathless, she slowed her pace and grinned at Salene.

Salene threw up her hands, and said, "All right, in footraces you beat me half the time."

"Only half?" Clara teased, smiling, and then she went quiet.

As they entered the gate to the Triune Hall, Clara always felt honored to simply be there. Today she felt even more awed than usual. She had been training for today her whole life. She felt as if time slowed around her, as she took in the scene around her.

Each stone of the Three Halls was carved with words and decorations, and each was kept clean by apprentices like Clara herself. The courtyard was paved with multi-colored slabs of stone, and there were three oases of gardens in the midst of it with grassy areas to sit, and trees to climb or pick fruit from depending on the season. The open blue sky above them, the scents of the blossoms, the sounds of the voices around them made Clara almost want to stop this moment in time forever. The anticipation and excitement building in her felt full and sweet in and of itself, and she tried to hold onto it.

She paused at the fountain in the courtyard and looked down into the shallow water which lapped gently against the marble sides. "I have been blessed."

Salene put her hand on Clara's shoulder and squeezed. "You've been dedicated to the way of the Sword for as long as I can remember. Remember when you greeted me with that stick and challenged me to a bout?"

Clara smiled ruefully. She had been a terror of the Desert Halls when she was growing up. "I don't think I'll ever forget that."

"Well, time to make a new memory," Salene encouraged her. She stepped away from the fountain and led the way into the vast entry hall.

Following her, Clara gazed up at the marble floor and tall columns, a far cry from the smaller and simpler Triune Hall structure in the Desert district. It made sense that the capital of Septily would have the most beautiful and largest of the Triune Halls, outfitted with a glorious cathedral, and special training areas for each of the three disciplines: The Sword, the Truth, and the Way, or better known as: The Sword Masters, the Law-Givers and The Shepherds, all bound together by their belief in one faith.

Clara knew that not everyone in Septily believed in the Lord, the Creator, Savior, and Spirit, but she couldn't imagine not believing. To believe in nothing made no sense to her, and to believe in a stone god made last year in a rock quarry didn't make sense to her either.

Salene broke into her thoughts with a squeeze on her

arm. "Hey, you're ready, you know that, right?"

"I think so," said Clara, realizing that she was nervous as well as excited.

"Then I'll see you at luncheon," Salene said, and she walked away, leaving Clara at the reception desk that stood between the Sword Master's Council Chamber and the Chamber of Choice.

Clara approached the reception desk, where a young sword guard she didn't recognize sat waiting.

"May I help you, apprentice?" he asked, in a voice thick with burr of the Forester province.

"Yes, thank you," Clara said. "I'm to meet Master Dantor here, and enter the Chamber of the Sword this morning."

He smiled at her, and then looked down at his papers. "You're expected," he said. "Although you're younger than I thought you would be."

Clara merely nodded, knowing that she was younger than most students who entered their mastership. At fifteen, she had already passed up students two to three years older than herself.

"You're to wait there, by the doors to the Chamber,"

said the sword guard.

"Thank you, sir," said Clara. She walked slowly over the doors, which were carved with several scenes, the history of the Champions of Septily. The first Champion, Champion Elar, overlapped the two doors at the center. Champion Elar had fought back the divisive forces of the Dark Sisterhood and brought seven kingdoms together to form Septily itself. The carving showed him standing in the midst of a map of Septily, fighting back a dark cloud over his head. She shivered at the sight of that cloud now, reminded of her nightmare.

Champion Elar had been called by the Lord to serve with King Wilstorm nearly two thousand years ago. Since then, four other Champions had been called to serve the country. Depictions of Champion Ferris, Champion Tamara, Champion Hest, and Champion Samuel ringed the one of Champion Elar. More space had been left on the doors for future carvings of future Champions.

From Clara's understanding there were Champions that showed up in other countries all over the world of Aramatir, and Clara had studied some of the legends about them as part of her training. Each Champion held a special place of honor in the Triune Halls, chosen by the Lord of all to be a light in the darkest times. The Triune Halls were an over-reaching form of government that transcended country boundaries, and knit the fabric of Aramatir together. The Champions upheld the highest values of faith, strength, loyalty, honor, and sacrifice.

Clara had tried to lose herself in the history of the Champions, but she felt the swell of anticipation in every moment. She had tried to focus on the details of the carving in front of her, but as time passed, she became more aware of her fast pulse and the lightness in her chest.

Finally, Master Dantor exited the Sword Council door to her left, and crossed the room towards her. His stern, lean face was furrowed in thought.

She saluted him, with her hand to her heart, and he returned the salute somberly.

He stood in front of her and observed her for a moment, then ran his hand over his short, dark hair and sighed.

Instantly cold sweat broke out on Clara's arms. Something had to be very wrong. Master Dantor didn't sigh without reason. She couldn't imagine what it could be. Her mind raced through everything that had happened during all the tests she had endured to reach the Mastery level of training. "Sir?" she said, not really knowing what to ask.

He took a deep breath and let it out slowly, and then nodded to himself. "Clara, do you know the legends of the Champions?"

Clara looked at the doors in front of her, as if they held the answers she needed to pass this final, and unexpected test. "I know them, Master Dantor."

Master Dantor followed her gaze, and smiled briefly. "I hope you know them beyond the depictions on those doors after all these years, Clara."

"Yes, sir," Clara said, feeling a little irritated now. Hadn't this been covered in the grilling interview she had completed just yesterday in the Sword Council chambers?

Master Dantor's dark eyes seemed to bore down on her, but Clara kept her poise and waited.

Dantor looked over at the doors again. "Some of the Shepherds are granted with visions from the Lord regarding the future of our land and the future of the Halls. Some have even seen glimpses of the next Champion."

Clara wanted to ask why this mattered to her, but she kept her silence. She knew that Dantor wasn't finished yet. He seemed as if he were leading to something.

"It is rare, but sometimes others receive visions of that kind. Many years ago, I had a vision of the next Champion. In my vision she was battle-stained and weary, although young in years. I had the vision confirmed by one of the Shepherds from the Hall of Wisdom, and as the years went by, I searched for her but never found her." He looked at her directly now, his eyes like coals against his tan, weather-beaten face. "Last night I had the same vision, and the Champion had your face."

NOTES

"DRAGONFOLD," first published in 2008 in Mind Flights online (http://www.mindflights.com/), was my first paid publication, and I still remember that awesome, jumping for joy moment. This story is dedicated to my mom, the Paper Lady. At one time in her life, she could fold over seventy origami figures from memory.

"THE IDENTITY OF CAPTAIN WRATH" was inspired by the Picture Paints a Thousand Words Blogfest hosted by Unicorn Bell (http://unicornbell.blogspot.com/).

"FIERCE LOVE" was written circa 2009.

"NEW GROWTH" is part of a series of stories about Sage and her mentor in 2009 and 2010.

"BATTLE CALL" was inspired Sensational Haiku Wednesday at You Know that Blog (http://youknowthatblog.com/), even though it didn't end up being a haiku. Previously published on my blog and at figment in 2012.

"ENOUGH TO DO" was first published in 2010 at Every Day Fiction online (http://www.everydayfiction.com/) and is the first of a series of stories.

"AT THE EDGE" was inspired by the Sacrifice Blog Hop in 2012 hosted by Sheena-kay Graham at Queendsheena (http://queendsheena.blogspot.com/).

"PTW FRED" came from a visit to a place on the Olympic coastline of Washington State aptly named the Hole in the Wall. It's only accessible at low tide, and is home to a beautiful array of sea life. Written in 2008.

"HAIKU – ROBOT" was inspired by a haiku contest in 2012 hosted by Nate Wilson at Sometimes, The Wheel is On Fire (http://wheelisonfire.blogspot.com/).

"WAR, INCORPORATED EXCERPT" is the second chapter of my first full length novel. I wrote the novel for the Commercial Fiction and Advanced Commercial Fiction classes at the University of Washington from 1999-2001. The first chapter was previously published in *New Voices IV* from Goodfellow Press, and is currently out of print.

"CAPTAIN WRATH GOES CAMPING" was inspired by the Lighting Flashed flash fiction blog fest hosted by Cherie Reich (http://cheriereich.blogspot.com/).

"EMBERS" was first published in 2010 in an online magazine called *Moon Drenched Fables*, which is sadly no longer in existence.

"ADRIFT" was written in 2011.

"RUBY RED" is a fractured fairy tale I wrote for a

specific anthology in 2008. It didn't make it in, but I kept revising it, and the current story is the result of that.

"CHAMELEONS" is one of the few stories that I can honestly say that I dreamed before writing back in 2009.

"HAIKU – SPACE #1 and #2" are a pair of poems that were inspired by a haiku contest in 2013 hosted by Nate Wilson at Sometimes, the Wheel is on Fire (http://wheelisonfire.blogspot.com/).

"INTERROGATION" was first published in *Overcoming Adversity: An Anthology for Andrew* in 2013, edited by Nick Wilford of Scattergun Scribblings (http://nickwilford.blogspot.com/). I highly recommend this anthology of stories by a variety of authors for a great cause.

"CHAMPION IN THE DARKNESS EXCERPT" is from my first published novel, Champion in the Darkness, published in 2013. For further reading, you can find it online at Amazon (http://www.amazon.com/Champion-Darkness-Trilogy-ebook/dp/B00BCD1YJA/ref=sr_1_1?s=books&ie=UTF8&qid=1370102570&sr=1-1&keywords=champion+in+the+darkness).

ABOUT THE AUTHOR

Tyrean Martinson lives and writes in the Pacific Northwest, encouraged by her multi-talented husband and daughters. She likes to write, read, teach, ski, bicycle, and walk.

Using her degree in Secondary Education with an emphasis in English, Tyrean homeschools her two daughters and teaches writing and literature classes at Harbor Christian Homeschool Co-operative.

Tyrean has been published in e-zines like *Every Day Poets*, *Every Day Fiction* and *Mindflights*, and a few print anthologies like *Overcoming Adversity*, *The Best of Every Day Poets* and *Sunday Snaps: The Stories*. *Champion in the Darkness* is the first book in The Champion Trilogy, and *Dragonfold and Other Adventures* is her first published collection.

Find Tyrean Martinson online:
Blog: http://tyreanswritingspot.blogspot.com/
Facebook https://www.facebook.com/pages/Tyrean-Martinson/71505118164
Twitter https://twitter.com/TyreanMartinson

www.ingramcontent.com/pod-product-compliance
Lightning Source LLC
Chambersburg PA
CBHW050755250626
47155CB00005B/2071